## ABOUT

Barbara Cartland, the wo... ...s also an historian, p... ...television personalit... ...sold over 600 million...

She has also had many... ...ritten four autobiograph... ...nother and that of her brother, Ronald Cartland, who was the first Member of Parliament to be killed in the last war. This book has a preface by Sir Winston Churchill and has just been published with an introduction by the late Sir Arthur Bryant.

"Love at the Helm" a novel written with the help and inspiration of the late Earl Mountbatten of Burma, Great Uncle of His Royal Highness The Prince of Wales, is being sold for the Mountbatten Memorial Trust.

She has broken the world record for the last seventeen years by writing an average of twenty-three books a year. In the Guinness Book of Records she is listed as the world's top-selling author.

In 1978 she sang an Album of Love Songs with the Royal Philharmonic Orchestra.

In private life Barbara Cartland, who is a Dame of Grace of the Order of St. John of Jerusalem, Chairman of the St. John Council in Hertfordshire and Deputy President of the St. John Ambulance Brigade, has fought for better conditions and salaries for Midwives and Nurses.

She championed the cause for the Elderly in 1956 invoking a Government Enquiry into the "Housing Conditions of Old People".

In 1962 she had the Law of England changed so that Local Authorities had to provide camps for their own Gypsies. This has meant that since then thousands and thousands of Gypsy children have been able to go to School which they had never been able to do in the past, as their caravans were moved every twenty-four hours by the Police.

There are now fourteen camps in Hertfordshire and Barbara Cartland has her own Romany Gypsy Camp called Barbaraville by the Gypsies.

Her designs "Decorating with Love" are being sold all over the USA and the National Home Fashions League made her in 1981, "Woman of Achievement".

Barbara Cartland's book "Getting Older, Growing Younger" has been published in Great Britain and the USA and her fifth Cookery Book, "The Romance of Food" is now being used by the House of Commons.

In 1984 she received at Kennedy Airport, America's Bishop Wright Air Industry Award for her contribution to the development of aviation. In 1931 she and two RAF Officers thought of, and carried the first aeroplane-towed glider air-mail.

During the War she was Chief Lady Welfare Officer in Bedfordshire looking after 20,000 Service men and women. She thought of having a pool of Wedding Dresses at the War Office so a service Bride could hire a gown for the day.

She bought 1,000 secondhand gowns without coupons for the ATS, the WAAFS and the WRENS. In 1945 Barbara Cartland received the Certificate of Merit from Eastern Command.

In 1964 Barbara Cartland founded the National Association for Health of which she is the President, as a front for all the Health Stores and for any product made as alternative medicine.

This has now a £500,000,000 turnover a year, with one third going in export.

In January 1988 she received "La Medaille de Vermeil de la Ville de Paris", (The Gold Medal of Paris). This is the highest award to be given by the City of Paris for ACHIEVE-MENT – 25 million books sold in France.

In March 1988 Barbara Cartland was asked by the Indian Government to open their Health Resort outside Delhi. This is almost the largest Health Resort in the world.

Barbara Cartland was received with great enthusiasm by her fans, who also fêted her at a Reception in the City and she received the gift of an embossed plate from the Government.

Barbara Cartland was made a Dame of the Order of the British Empire in the 1991 New Year's Honours List, by Her Majesty The Queen for her contribution to literature and for her work for the Community.

# AWARDS

1945  Received Certificate of Merit, Eastern Command.

1953  Made a Commander of the Order of St. John of Jerusalem. Invested by H.R.H. The Duke of Gloucester at Buckingham Palace.

1972  Invested as Dame of Grace of the Order of St. John in London by The Lord Prior, Lord Cacia.

1981  Receives "Achiever of the Year" from the National Home Furnishing Association in Colorado Springs, U.S.A.

1984  Receives Bishop Wright Air Industry Award at Kennedy Airport, for inventing the aeroplane-towed Glider.

1988  Receives from Monsieur Chirac, The Prime Minister, the Gold Medal of the City of Paris, at the Hôtel de la Ville, Paris, for selling 25 million books and giving a lot of employment.

1991  Invested as Dame of the Order of The British Empire, by H.M. The Queen at Buckingham Palace, for her contribution to literature.

Novella is in the hall of her Father's house when to her astonishment a man runs up the drive, tears into the hall and says:

"Save me! Save me! If you cannot hide me they will kill me!"

Because she is quick-witted she realised that he is a Gentleman and also that he has been shot in the arm and the blood is running down his hand.

She hides him in the Secret Passage which was used centuries ago by the Catholics escaping from the wrath of Queen Elizabeth and later the Royalists and the Cromwellians.

Just as she has got him hidden, a man called Lord Grimstone arrives, who was always disliked by her Father, a General fighting in Wellington's Army.

Lord Grimstone demands that he shall search the house, but Novella refuses to allow him to do so, as her Mother is ill.

Only when he has tried every way to make her change her mind, does Grimstone realise how attractive Novella is and talks to her in a very different way.

Finally he leaves but she is aware that his spies are watching the house so that they can kill the stranger if he appears. He however, is suffering from a high temperature from his wound, and is nursed by Nanny and the old Butler.

He is ill for some time and when he is well enough to talk he begs Novella to go to London with a very secret and important message for Viscount Palmerston who is the Secretary of State for War.

Novella agrees and she takes the coded message only to find that she is being watched on the journey by Lord Grimstone's spies.

How she discovers how important the stranger whose life

she has saved. How she undertakes to do something for Viscount Palmerston and the Prime Minister which for her is particularly dangerous, and how eventually she is saved by the stranger is all told in this thrilling and exciting 510th novel by Barbara Cartland.

# BARBARA CARTLAND

# Love Runs In

Mandarin

**A Mandarin Paperback**

LOVE RUNS IN

First published in Great Britain 1996
by Mandarin Paperbacks
an imprint of Reed International Books Ltd
Michelin House, 81 Fulham Road, London SW3 6RB
and Auckland, Melbourne, Singapore and Toronto

Copyright © Cartland Promotions 1996

The author has asserted her moral rights

A CIP catalogue record for this title
is available from the British Library
ISBN 0 7493 1273 4

Phototypeset by Intype London Ltd
Printed and bound in Great Britain
by Cox & Wyman Ltd, Reading, Berks.

# AUTHOR'S NOTE

As I have told in this novel when the War with Napoleon Bonaparte became more and more intense as it drew to an end, he considered the English Smugglers to be his friends.

He even, at one time, established a special camp for them on the coast at Gravelines.

It was believed that the Smugglers also carried War secrets and French spies across the Channel and there is no doubt that given a sufficient amount of money they would take home French Prisoners of War who had escaped.

Jack Rattenbury a notorious West Country smuggler was caught and found to have agreed to take four French Officers across for £100.

The money that Napoleon received for the goods brought back by the Smugglers was always in gold and enabled him to buy extra arms from the few countries in Europe who were not yet at war.

When finally Napoleon Bonaparte was banished into exile on St. Helena his friends approached the famous English smuggler Thomas Johnson and offered him a bribe of £40,000 if he could arrange to rescue the Emperor.

# CHAPTER ONE
## 1813

Novella trotted her horse into the stables and dismounted.

There was no one about and she thought the groom was probably working in the garden.

As they were very short-staffed owing to the war, everybody left behind was doing two jobs, rather than one.

She put her horse in his stall and unfastened his saddle.

Placing it on the bar in the passage she went back for the bridle.

Then she checked to see that there was food in the manger and fresh water in the pail.

"You have been a good boy!" she said. "If there is time, we will go out again this afternoon."

As she patted him she felt sure that *Heron* understood what she was saying to him.

He nuzzled against her before she left.

Walking back to the house she thought it was a lovely day, and it was a pity that she had so much to do indoors.

Her Mother was ill.

Although Nanny, in spite of getting old, was a tremendous help, there were still dozens of things for her to do.

Lady Wentmore was unable to leave her bedroom.

As Novella came from the stable-yard in sight of the house, she felt as she saw her home, a little thrill run through her.

Nothing, she thought, could be more lovely.

The bricks which had turned pink with age, the gabled roofs and the strange chimneys which were characteristic of the Elizabethan era.

The house had been in the hands of the Wentmore family for generations.

Her Father, who was fighting in the Peninsula with Wellington must, she thought, be longing day after day to see it again.

"If only this ghastly war was over," Novella told herself, "we could all be together and happy as we used to be."

She felt a pang of fear go through her in case her Father was killed.

There had been so many casualties in the village.

She knew that her Mother's illness was partially due to the fact that she was afraid she might never see her husband again.

Novella reached the centre of the ancient hall with its huge medieval fireplace and panelled walls.

As she did so she heard an unexpected sound behind her.

She turned in surprise.

She was then aware that what she had heard was the sound of running feet. Someone was moving at a tremendous pace across the gravelled Courtyard.

Before she could wonder what was happening, a man dashed up the steps and into the hall.

She looked at him in astonishment.

He was not one of their neighbours, but a stranger.

He was handsome, young, and obviously a gentleman.

However he looked at the moment somewhat dishevelled.

When he saw her standing and staring at him, he came to a standstill and said:

"For God's sake, hide me! If they catch me, they will kill me!"

Novella gave a gasp of amazement.

Then she saw that blood was running down his arm and over his hand.

"They have shot me in the arm," he said, "and the next time they shoot I will be dead!"

As he spoke he looked over his shoulder apprehensively.

Novella knew that the man from whom he was running away could not be far behind.

With a swiftness of decision that was characteristic of her she said:

"Come with me!"

She passed through the hall and started to run down a long passage which led to the Library.

She opened the door, aware that the stranger was just behind her.

He was still breathing heavily, as he had done when he first came into the house.

The Library was a beautiful room with books lining the walls. Halfway up one wall there ran a gallery which was reached by curving steps.

The room also contained a large medieval fireplace, but to this had been added later a marble mantelpiece.

As Novella looked at it, she thought she heard a sound from the hall which they had just left.

She went quickly to the side of the mantelpiece and pressed one of the carved flowers in the oak panelling.

A narrow door slid open.

"A secret passage!" the stranger beside her exclaimed. "That is exactly what I need. Thank you, thank you, for saving my life!"

Even as he was speaking, he bent his head and climbed through the dark opening.

"Keep to the left," Novella whispered, "and you will come to the Priest's room."

She closed the panelling.

Moving away from the fireplace she crossed to the other side of the room.

Even as she did so, she knew that somebody was coming down the passage.

The next minute the door that had been left ajar was thrown open.

A man was standing there whom she recognised.

It was Lord Grimstone whose Castle was about a mile away overlooking the sea.

Novella had seen him in the hunting-field and at the Lord Lieutenant's Garden Party she had twice attended with her Mother.

She could not remember his ever coming to the Hall and knew it was because her Father did not like him.

Moreover Lord Grimstone, she had always heard, himself had no desire to associate with his neighbours.

Because of this she thought it a gross impertinence that he should have walked into the house without being admitted by a servant.

A man of over forty, he had been good-looking when he was young.

Now his face was debauched, with heavy lines under his eyes and dark lines running from his nose to his chin.

"Where is he?" he asked in a sharp domineering tone.

Novella looked at him in surprise.

"I think, Sir," she said slowly, "that you are Lord Grimstone. I have heard my Father speak of you, but we have not met."

"Where is that man I saw coming into the house?" Lord Grimstone demanded.

"Man?" Novella repeated. "I do not know what you mean unless you are referring to Dawkins our man-servant."

"I am not talking about servants," Lord Grimstone retorted angrily, "but the man who escaped from the fools who were trying to capture him. I know he is somewhere in this house!"

"I am afraid you are mistaken, My Lord," Novella replied. "As my Mother is unwell and my Father fighting with Lord Wellington, we are not receiving guests at the moment."

"I am not a guest dammit!" Lord Grimstone shouted.

Then as he saw the shocked expression on Novella's face, he added hastily:

"Forgive me, I should not have sworn in front of a Lady. At the same time, it is infuriating that I should have lost this man."

"I cannot imagine who you are talking about,

My Lord," Novella said, "but I assure you, whoever it is you are pursuing, he is not here!"

"I am quite certain he is!" Lord Grimstone retorted. "And I insist my men must search for him."

Novella drew herself up.

"This is my home," she said, "and, as I have already told Your Lordship, my Mother is ill. I cannot believe you would behave in this extremely aggressive manner if my Father were at home."

"The General would certainly not frustrate me by preventing my men from looking for this fellow," Lord Grimstone argued.

"My Father would ask the reason why you are hunting this man, and would also make it clear to you that he is not in this house."

Because she was lying, which was something she never did, she crossed her fingers.

She was telling herself at the same time that she could not and would not hand over the man she had hidden to anyone as despicable and unpleasant as Lord Grimstone.

"Whatever you may say," he said now, "I intend to find this man and arrest him!"

"Then you had better look elsewhere," Novella said, "for I cannot have your men disturbing my Mother by trampling all over the place. In any case, it is an outrage that they should do so without my permission."

Lord Grimstone realised this was true.

He stood for a moment irresolute, but obviously determined somehow to find his prey.

Then, unexpectedly, and in a very different voice he looked at Novella and said:

"You have grown since I last saw you, into a very pretty young woman."

He looked her up and down in a way that was insulting.

Lifting her chin a little higher, she said:

"If I am not mistaken, My Lord, I think I can hear your men walking about in the hall. Kindly tell them to remain outside until we have finished our conversation."

She spoke with a dignity that made her seem older than her years.

She walked past Lord Grimstone and along the passage.

She did so unhurriedly and without looking behind her to see if he was following.

He looked round the Library, then with an oath under his breath left the room.

When Novella reached the hall he was not far behind her.

She found three men looking under the stairs, behind a chest and a grandfather-clock.

Then they were peering upwards towards the landing.

In the same tone she had used to Lord Grimstone she said:

"As you have not been invited into this house, will you kindly wait outside until you have permission to enter."

The men she thought were a rough type, and not in any way characteristic of the Locals.

They looked at her in surprise.

Then somewhat sheepishly they moved towards the front door.

They had just reached it when Lord Grimstone appeared.

They stopped and looked towards him as if awaiting his orders.

"Do as the Lady said!" he commanded. "I will call you when you are wanted."

They touched their caps which they had not removed and walked down the steps into the courtyard.

Lord Grimstone stopped in front of the fireplace.

"Now, look here, my girl," he said, "you must not stand in the way of justice. I insist on taking the man who is somewhere in this house away with me."

"If you are speaking of justice, My Lord," Novella replied, "I imagine that is something which should be discussed with the Chief Constable, whom my Father knows well. If you will fetch him and tell him what this trouble is all about, I will of course co-operate with him in any way that he requires."

Novella saw by the expression on Lord Grimstone's face that the last thing he wanted was the Chief Constable interfering in what he was doing.

She had played a trump-card to which he had no answer.

Yet as if he was not to be defeated by a mere girl, he said:

"There is no need to make all this fuss about it! I had the man arrested and he escaped. All I want to do is to search the house and take him away to where he will cause no more trouble."

"That is something which to my knowledge this unknown stranger has not done," Novella said. "I find Your Lordship's behaviour extraordinary, and something I have never encountered before!"

For a moment Lord Grimstone looked slightly embarrassed.

Then he said:

"You are being very clever in getting your own way, but I am determined not to leave empty-handed."

"Very well," Novella said. "If you insist, your men can search the house so long as they do not disturb my Mother."

She paused before continuing.

"But I think my Father will have something to say about Your Lordship's behaviour. I shall certainly inform him of it as soon as he returns home from fighting for his country against Napoleon Bonaparte."

As she spoke she walked away and opened the door which led into the Drawing-Room.

Her heart was beating frantically as she moved towards the bow-window which overlooked the rose-garden.

Yet she thought she had behaved in the way her Father would have expected her to do.

She hoped that for the moment Lord Grimstone was completely nonplussed.

He had in fact watched her leave.

Then, as if against his better judgement he had been convinced by what Novella said, he went to the front door.

His men were standing below the steps.

Lord Grimstone's Phaeton was behind them and a Brake in which he had intended to carry his prisoner away was just coming more slowly up the drive.

Standing at the top of the steps Lord Grimstone said to his men in a harsh voice:

"You are quite certain the man we are seeking came in here?"

One of them who looked a little more intelligent than the other two, said:

"Oi thinks 'e done, M'Lord, but 'e might've slipped away round t'the side o' t'house. We was a long ways from 'im, as Yer Lordship rightly knows."

Lord Grimstone frowned.

"I might have guessed you would make a mess of it!" he said sullenly. "Well, search the garden you fools! If he is not in the house, that is where he must be hiding."

The men hurried to obey him.

They ran round to the side of the house, peering behind the yew-hedges and bushes.

Novella was watching them from the window in the Drawing-Room.

She had a feeling of triumph at having outwitted Lord Grimstone.

At the same time, she could not help wondering what the stranger had done that had resulted in his being taken prisoner.

Had she been mistaken and was he really a dangerous criminal?

He had appealed to her for sanctuary.

She had therefore been determined that she would not hand him over to anyone so unpleasant as Lord Grimstone.

'Perhaps when he has gone, I should send for the Chief Constable,' she thought.

It was essential first to make certain that Lord Grimstone had really left.

He must not be spying on her when she released the man who was now in the secret passage.

Ever since she had been a child, Novella had loved the secret passages which her Father had shown her.

He had told her stories about those who had hidden there.

When the house was first built by his ancestor, Catholics who were persecuted by the followers of Queen Elizabeth had been saved.

Then during the Civil War the house had been searched time and time again by Cromwellian troops hunting out Royalists.

Novella had invented stories in which she had to hide from Giants or goblins who were pursuing her.

However, she had never expected in real life to hide a man who was in danger of losing his life.

'As soon as Lord Grimstone is gone, I must talk to the Stranger', she thought, 'and also take him a bandage for his arm.'

She was sure it must be very painful.

She watched the men in the garden roughly pulling apart the shrubs.

They would be just as rough, she thought, with the man who had escaped them if they found him.

The three men, having looked around the garden were now conversing with each other.

They then shrugged their shoulders as if they realised their prey was lost and there was nothing they could do about it.

It was then that she heard Lord Grimstone say behind her:

"Those idiots have lost the man for the moment, but make no mistake about it, I shall capture him sooner or later."

Novella turned round.

"I can only hope, My Lord, that it will not be on my Father's Estate. If you should call here again, perhaps you would be kind enough to give us notice of your visit. Or at least, if you arrive unexpectedly, knock on the door."

As she finished speaking she realised that Lord Grimstone was astounded that she should have spoken to him in such a way.

Then unexpectedly he laughed.

"At least you have pluck, my girl!" he said. "I suppose because you are so pretty you think you can get away with it!"

Again he was appraising her.

As his eyes roved over her body Novella had the idea that he was mentally undressing her.

She dropped him a small curtsey saying:

"Would you be so kind, My Lord, as to tell your coachman to shut the main gates after him. The gate-keeper is in the Army, and his wife suffers from rheumatism."

Once again Lord Grimstone laughed.

"We must meet again, Miss Wentmore," he said, "in happier circumstances. Perhaps you would care to dine with me one evening? I would send my carriage for you."

"Thank you, My Lord," Novella replied stiffly "but while my Mother is so ill it is impossible for me to leave her."

Lord Grimstone's lips twitched.

"I am not a man to take no for an answer," he said. "I will concede to you my prisoner, as we cannot find him here, but I promise you I shall see you again, and very shortly."

He walked towards the door with a swagger.

He then looked back as if he expected Novella to follow him.

Once again she made a small bob which was more of an insult than a curtsey.

Breathing heavily, Lord Grimstone walked across the hall and down the steps.

Novella did not move until she heard his Phaeton driving away, followed by the Brake.

Only when she could no longer hear them did she go to the front door.

Now she could see the Brake at the far end of the drive.

The Phaeton had already gone through the gates and onto the road that led through the village.

She wondered if perhaps Lord Grimstone had left one of his men behind to spy on the house.

She looked in the bushes that bordered the court-yard.

There did not appear to be anybody hiding in them.

Nevertheless she shut the front door and looked out, before she walked towards the Library.

Taking no chances she went first to the windows to make certain there was no one peeping in from the garden.

She had an impulse to draw the curtains, but she thought that would be a mistake.

She would certainly arouse suspicion if there was anybody outside.

She looked out of each of the three windows very carefully.

The birds were fluttering undisturbed over the lawn.

The white pigeons her Mother loved were moving amongst the flower-beds.

Novella thought that if a stranger was near them they would be fluttering away in alarm.

Finally, when quite some time had passed since Lord Grimstone had left, she went to the panelling.

The secret door opened, but there was no one waiting just inside.

Because she was still nervous, she went back into the Library.

She transferred the key from the outside of the door to the inside, and locked it.

She then put her head inside the entrance to the secret passage.

"Are you there?" she called softly.

There was no answer.

She supposed the Stranger had, as she had suggested, gone to the Priest's Room, which was where the Catholics had secretly said Mass.

It was some way from the entrance in the Library.

She knew how dark the passage was, although there were places where some light and air filtered in.

She therefore lit a candle on the mantelpiece and carried it into the secret passage.

She closed the secret panel behind her.

She walked slowly, shading the candle with her hand.

She did not wish it to be extinguished by an unexpected draught.

That was what had happened once with her Father.

They had to grope their way back to the entrance with some difficulty in the darkness.

She reached the Priest's Room.

It was small, but large enough to contain an altar that had a gold crucifix on it, and a prie-dieu.

There were also some needlepoint cushions on which to kneel, which were almost threadbare.

For a moment Novella thought there was no one there.

Then, lifting the candle, she saw slumped on the floor the man she had befriended.

His head was resting on the stool of the prie-dieu.

His eyes were closed, and for one frightening second she thought he was dead.

Then she realised he was just asleep.

The wound in his arm was bleeding onto the sleeve of his jacket.

For a few seconds she stared at him.

Then as if she called to him without speaking, he opened his eyes.

Novella gave a little sigh of relief as he said:

"Forgive me, but I have not slept for two nights, and I fell asleep without realising it."

"Lord Grimstone and his men have gone," Novella said, "but he was very unpleasant, and determined to find you."

"I thought he would be," the Stranger replied. "Now, how can I thank you for befriending me and saving my life?"

"Would he .. really have .. killed you?" Novella asked in a low voice.

"Undoubtedly!" the Stranger replied, "and as you see, they have already damaged my arm."

He looked down ruefully at the blood which covered his hand.

"It must be bandaged," Novella said, "and I

think it would be safe now for you to come out from here."

The Stranger got to his feet.

"Are you sure of that?" he asked. "If His Lordship is keen to get me, he will certainly have left a spy to watch in case I come out from my hiding-place."

"I thought of that," Novella replied, "and I looked through all the windows in the Library, but I am certain there is nobody there."

"Then I would be extremely grateful if I could wash," the Stranger said, "and if it is not too difficult for you, have something to eat."

Novella looked at him with concern.

"Where can you have been that you have not slept or eaten for so long?"

The Stranger hesitated.

"I . . I am sorry," Novella added quickly. "I was not meaning to . . pry and of course in the circumstances you will want to be as secretive as possible."

"Not with you," the Stranger replied, "when you have been so unbelievably kind."

His voice deepened as he added:

"I know of few women who would have acted so swiftly when I appealed for help, without asking innumerable questions before they revealed the perfect hiding-place."

He looked round the Priest's Room and said:

"It has always disappointed me that my own house does not contain a secret passage, or a Priest's Room like this. I can feel the sanctity of those who prayed here, generations ago."

Novella smiled.

"That is what I always feel when I come here,"

she said. "They were fighting for their faith, and their sincerity will live on for as long as the house stands."

"When I fell asleep," the Stranger said, "I felt as if a hand was touching my forehead and telling me I was safe."

"You must be very, very careful," Novella warned. "Lord Grimstone is a horrible man. My Father never liked him, and he will try to take you unawares."

"That is something I intend to avoid by every means within my power," the Stranger said, "but I do not wish to involve you in this unpleasant affair when you have been so kind to me."

"We can talk about that when I have bandaged your arm," Novella said. "Let us go back to the Library, and if we then go upstairs, it will be impossible for Lord Grimstone to appear without our being aware that he is in the house."

"I cannot tell you how grateful I am," the Stranger said quietly.

Novella turned towards the door, holding the candle high so that he could see the way and follow her.

She moved slowly back down the secret passage.

As she did so she thought this was the most exciting thing that had ever happened to her.

# CHAPTER TWO

When they reached the Library the panel was open and Novella stepped through it.

The Stranger followed her, then as he straightened himself he stumbled.

She realised that, though he had been talking sensibly since he awoke, he was in fact completely exhausted.

Without saying anything, she went ahead along the passage which led to the hall.

Only when she reached the staircase did she ask anxiously:

"D . . do you think you can . . climb the stairs?"

"Yes – of course," he answered. "I am – all right – only a – little tired."

She knew that was a very mild way of putting it.

She went up the stairs and was aware that as he followed her he was dragging himself up by the banisters.

He was holding his injured arm against his body.

Novella was relieved to see that although it was still bleeding, the blood was not actually dripping onto the floor.

As she reached the landing, Nanny came from her Mother's bedroom.

She looked in surprise at the Stranger.

"I was just looking for you, Nanny," Novella said. "This Gentleman has been shot in the arm and is bleeding badly. He is also extremely tired and I think should go to bed as soon as possible."

As usual, Nanny rose to the occasion.

"If you'll come this way, Sir . . " she said.

As she spoke she opened the door of a room that was just beyond Lady Wentmore's.

It was one kept for visiting gentlemen who her Father had entertained before he went to the war.

The decoration and furniture were somehow masculine, but the bed was large and comfortable.

As he went in through the door the Stranger staggered again and Nanny said sharply:

"Run downstairs, Miss Novella, get me a kettle of hot water, and ask Mr. Dawkins to come here at once."

Because Novella realised that Nanny in her usual way, had taken over she did as she was told.

When she reached the Kitchen, Dawkins was sitting at the table while his wife was busy at the stove.

"Nanny wants you upstairs," Novella told him. "We have a visitor who has been injured."

Dawkins rose slowly to his feet.

"I'll go up an' see what I can do," he said.

"Tell Nanny I will bring up a kettle of water as soon as it has boiled," Novella said.

He went from the Kitchen and Mrs. Dawkins exclaimed:

"An' who's bin shootin' who, I'd like to know!"

Novella thought it was something she wanted to know herself.

But she answered:

"I think it was an accident and the Gentleman, as well as being exhausted, is also very hungry."

As that was Mrs. Dawkins' province, she said:

"It won't take me a minute to make him some soup to start with, an' as the eggs have just come in, I'll cook him an omelette."

"I am sure he will appreciate that," Novella said. "And, please Mrs. Dawkins, may I have the kettle, as Nanny wishes to clean his wound."

Mrs. Dawkins pushed the kettle on to the centre of the stove where it would boil more quickly.

As soon as the water began to boil she handed it to Novella.

"Tell Nanny, Miss Novella," she said, "Oi'll be up with the soup in a jiffy, an' that's no s'aggeration!"

Novella smiled.

She was used to Mrs. Dawkins' funny way of saying things.

By the time she reached the bedroom she found that Nanny and Dawkins had got the Stranger into bed.

His wounded arm was resting on a pile of towels.

Now that she could see him more clearly Novella was aware that he was in fact very handsome and he was certainly well born.

It seemed strange to be entertaining a man whose name she did not know and who had appealed to her to save his life.

However she had little time to speculate about him.

Nanny sent her in search of bandages and healing creams.

Nanny made them from the flowers and herbs in the garden.

She had treated Novella with them ever since she was a child.

It took a little time for her to find everything Nanny required.

When she returned to the bedroom the Stranger had drunk his soup and was eating a little of the omelette.

She saw however that his eyes were half-shut.

As soon as Nanny had finished bandaging his arm his eyes were closed, and he seemed unaware that they were there.

Nanny pulled down the blinds and said to him as if speaking to a child:

"Now, you go to sleep, Sir, an' you'll feel better when you wake up."

The Stranger did not reply and Nanny bustled Novella out of the room.

When she had shut the door behind her she said:

"That gentleman's going to run a high temperature before the day's out."

"A temperature?" Novella exclaimed. "From the wound in his arm?"

"The bullet didn't touch the bone," Nanny said, "but he's lost a lot of blood, and unless I'm mistaken, his temperature's going up, and it'll be a day or two before he feels himself again."

Novella had never known Nanny to be wrong where illness was concerned.

She therefore gave a little sigh.

It was infuriating to think she would know no more of the mystery of the Stranger's arrival until perhaps the day after tomorrow.

As if Nanny could read her thoughts she said:

"An' who is he, if I may enquire?"

Novella smiled.

"The only thing I know about him," she replied, "is that he is an enemy of Lord Grimstone."

"Oh, that man!" Nanny exclaimed. "If your Father were here he wouldn't have him in the house!"

"I know that," Novella said. "And I think it was Lord Grimstone who shot the poor Gentleman."

"I've never heard such goings on," Nanny said. "It's a nasty wound, but thank the Lord I managed to get it clean."

Novella knew that Nanny always fussed in case any scratch or wound that she or anyone else received might become septic.

"I am sure he will recover in your capable hands, Nanny," she said.

She went downstairs to make quite certain that the secret panel had been properly closed before they left the Library.

If Lord Grimstone came in search of his quarry again, they might have to use it.

"I wonder who he is and why anybody would want to shoot him?" she puzzled.

Then she gave a little laugh that was like the chirping of a bird and added:

"It is exciting, very exciting, that something like this should be happening to me!"

. . . . . . .

Novella had never expected too much of life because she had grown up all through the war.

Her Father had been away fighting and her Mother was desperately unhappy.

As she grew older she realised the terrible effect the war had on everyone and everything around her.

The young men in the village were killed and the old men who had retired had to go back to work to keep alive.

There were shortages of almost everything one wanted from clothes to food.

She had believed that when she was grown up, in other words when she was eighteen, things would be different.

By that time the young men she had known as children were no longer to be found in the neighbourhood.

Days had often passed when no one came to the house and there was no one to talk to except her Mother and Nanny.

One thing that kept her happy was the horses.

*Heron*, the one she rode herself she loved dearly as if he was a brother.

She talked to him and told him how difficult things were and he seemed to understand.

She loved riding him through the woods.

She would hear the birds singing, the rabbits moving about in the undergrowth.

The sun was shining overhead.

It seemed impossible to believe that the English Army was fighting desperately against a monster who had conquered nearly all of Europe.

Yet when she saw her Mother's eyes when the postman came day after day and there was nothing from her Father it was then Novella realised how frightened Lady Wentmore was that she would never see her husband again.

Because she was so much alone, Novella had

no idea how beautiful she had grown in the last few years.

Her Mother had always been a beauty from the time she had made her *début*.

When she married she had been acclaimed the most beautiful bride of the Season.

While she resembled her Mother, Novella was distinctive.

She had a look about her which was very rare in a young woman.

It was not only a look of innocence and purity which every young man wanted in the woman he loved but there was also something spiritual about her.

It made her appear to the Stranger when she saved his life that she had just stepped down from Heaven.

Novella however had no idea of this.

She could not help feeling that however dramatic and frightening it might be there was certainly something unusual.

Day after day had gone by for months without there being anything new to include in the letters she wrote to her Father.

She told him everything that occurred.

Yet sometimes it was difficult to fill even one sheet of writing paper let alone several.

Now she thought with a sense of satisfaction she would have something sensational to tell him.

It would not only surprise him but would also be worth reading.

She was tired of writing '*the crops are just beginning to appear and we hope for a good season.*'

She would look down at what she had scribed

and hope her Father would not find it as boring as she did.

Then she remembered he had asked her particularly to send him every detail she possibly could.

About the house, the garden, the Estate and of course her Mother.

It was difficult to know what to say about that.

Her Mother grew paler and thinner.

She seemed to take little interest in anything except the letters which occasionally came from abroad.

These were few and far between.

Novella knew she put them under her pillow and she was sure that when no one was there her Mother kissed them again and again.

When she went to Church she would pray that the war would end soon.

If for no other reason but because it would bring her Mother so much happiness.

'How can she go on living without Papa,' she asked herself, 'and be frightened every day she may hear he has been killed?'

She wished sometimes there was someone with whom she could discuss the war which might make things better.

If she went to the village it was not unusual to hear that one of the younger men had been killed at sea or on the Peninsula.

There was really nothing she could say to comfort his weeping Mother.

The war, the war, it was always the war.

She thought of Napoleon Bonaparte with a loathing which seemed to dominate everything else she felt.

This included missing her Father desperately.

It hurt to see his empty chair at the table.

To know his study was shut up because he was no longer in it.

"The war, the war," she said again, "and we are so on the outside of it that I almost feel ashamed that there is nothing I can do to help."

Then suddenly out of the blue when she was least expecting it a Stranger had come running in to beg her help.

Then the house was invaded by the ghastly Lord Grimstone.

Could he really contemplate killing a young man and how could he behave in such an outrageous manner?

'No one,' Novella thought had ever behaved in such a way all the time she had been growing up.

She had a feeling when she went to bed that the whole thing was part of her imagination.

It could not actually be true.

She had gone down to the Library to make sure the panel door was shut.

Then she saw there were spots of blood on the carpet.

Quickly she cleaned them away.

Fortunately they did not show up on the Persian design.

She knew however if Lord Grimstone had seen them he might have behaved very differently.

Whatever she might have said he would have refused to leave the house.

As she cleaned away the blood, she thought Nanny must be very careful in throwing away the blood-stained bandages.

They would certainly be evidence that something unusual was happening inside the Hall if they were discovered.

If anyone had even the slightest idea that a wounded man had run up the drive and sought sanctuary from his pursuers, she could imagine only too clearly how people would talk in the village.

'It would keep them chatting for a month!' Novella told herself.

She was well aware that it was something which must not happen under any circumstances.

However aggressive Lord Grimstone might appear he was not completely convinced that she was lying.

Although he might watch the Hall there was no reason he should know the Stranger was in bed and being tended by Nanny.

Unless of course the servants talked!

She was quite certain Dawkins and his wife would not do so.

They adored her Father and would do everything in their power to make the war come to an end.

They would be discretion itself.

Lord Grimstone would have to look for some other sign to convince him.

First the man he wanted was alive.

Second that he was wounded and being looked after in the safety of Wentmore Hall.

Everything to do with his wound must be burned, Novella told herself.

She thought she would discuss this with Dawkins, his wife and Nanny.

The one person who must not be upset or have any idea what was occurring was her Mother.

She must not be worried.

As she grew weaker it was very important she should sleep well and not be concerned with trivial matters.

'It was enough for her to be worrying about Papa' Novella thought.

There was no reason for her Mother to fuss over a Stranger!

She had however to admit she was curious to know who he was.

It was quite obvious he was a Gentleman.

He was extremely athletic.

To be able to run so far having been shot in the arm was an achievement which most men would find impossible.

Perhaps tomorrow I shall be able to talk to him, Novella told herself and felt excited at the idea.

At last when she least expected it something was happening.

She knew almost as if someone had told her so, nothing was going to be quite the same in the future.

· · · · · · ·

As Nanny had predicted he developed a very high temperature.

When Novella went to see him the following day he still looked very flushed.

Nanny's instructions were that she should stay only a few minutes.

She went to the bedside and sitting down on a chair she asked:

"How do you feel?"

"I am worried – and I do not know what to do about it," the Stranger replied.

"Do about what?" Novella enquired.

He hesitated, she thought, as if he was feeling for words.

Finally he said:

"I have to get a message to London, and although I should go myself, I have the feeling that your Nanny is just as strict as mine was, and will prevent me from doing so."

"Of course she will," Novella replied. "You still have a temperature, and she says your arm is hurting you."

"It is certainly very painful," the Stranger agreed, "but I must make an effort to go tomorrow."

Novella shook her head.

"I am sure Nanny will not let you do anything of the sort."

The Stranger smiled.

"With anyone else I would go on my own, but as I have already said, your Nanny is just like mine."

Novella laughed.

Then knowing he was really worried she asked:

"Could not someone else go to London for you?"

"Who?" the Stranger asked abruptly.

Novella thought.

It was doubtful if Abbey the old Groom in the stables had ever been out of the village.

The two boys who assisted him with the horses were much too young.

There might be someone in the village.

It was then the Stranger said sharply:

"No one outside this house must know I am

here! If Grimstone knows where I am he will not miss me another time."

"So it was Lord Grimstone who shot you!" Novella exclaimed.

"Fortunately I moved as he did so, otherwise he would have hit me in the heart, as he intended."

"But .. why? Why should he .. do such a thing?" Novella asked.

The Stranger did not answer and after a moment she said:

"I .. I am not .. trying to .. pry .. or ask uncomfortable questions which you .. cannot answer .. "

"You are kindness itself," the Stranger said, "and I hate to impose on you."

The way he spoke made her say hesitatingly:

"Do you .. want me to .. go to .. London for you?"

"It is wrong of me to suggest such a thing," the Stranger said, "but I think, as a soldier's daughter, you will understand."

"I suppose Nanny told you who my Father is," Novella said.

"She told me, and of course I know the General by reputation. He would certainly understand the urgency of the message which I must get to the Secretary of State for War."

Novella's eyes widened.

"It is as important as that?"

"If it reaches him in time, it may save the lives of a great number of our men," the Stranger said simply.

Novella drew in her breath.

"In which case, you know I will take it to him."

As she spoke she was thinking wildly how she

could manage to go all the way to London without having somebody to go with her.

She needed someone who would not talk.

Nor think it strange that she should want to go to London for no apparent reason.

"Of course you cannot go alone," the Stranger said as if he was following her thoughts. "I have a feeling you are looking after your Mother, and anyway Nanny would never let you go on your own."

"That is true," Novella admitted.

She gave a sudden cry.

"I know who would accompany me! My old Governess, Miss Graham lives in the next village. Like Nanny she will take care of me as if I was still a small child."

"That is exactly the sort of person I would want you to have with you," the Stranger said. "Have you as many horses as you will need on such a journey?"

"We would have to change twice at Posting Inns," Novella said.

"Then – you will really go?" the Stranger asked.

"Of course I will, if it is as important as you say it is," Novella answered.

"Then I can only thank you from the bottom of my heart," he said in a deep voice. "Now, if it is possible, I would like to write down what you have to take with you, so I require pen, writing-paper and ink."

"I will fetch them for you," Novella said, "but do you think you ought to move? It may start your wound bleeding again."

"If it does, Nanny will stop it," the Stranger answered.

Because it was what she thought herself, Novella gave a little laugh.

She ran down the stairs.

Going to her Father's Study, she collected his blotter, writing-paper, ink and a quill-pen.

She took it to the Stranger and helped him to sit up in bed.

She realised that it hurt him to do so.

It was fortunately his left arm that had been wounded.

She arranged the blotter and the writing-paper in front of him and set the ink-pot on a book to keep it steady.

Having done so she said a little shyly:

"I have tried not to be inquisitive .. but I think .. if I am to go to London .. I should at least know your name."

The Stranger stared at her. Then he exclaimed:

"Good heavens! It never occurred to me that you had no idea who I am! Of course, it was exceedingly remiss of me not to introduce myself!"

Novella waited and after a moment he said:

"My name is Vale Chester, but it is a name that must not be spoken outside this room. When you get to London, you must just refer to me as 'One-Five'."

Novella's eyes opened wide.

"You mean .. you are doing something very secret" she asked.

"Very, very secret," Vale Chester agreed. "And that is why no one, Novella, except you, must be aware of my name."

Novella had noticed that he used her Christian name, and she therefore said:

"Perhaps it would be safer if I referred to you here as Mr. 'Vale', and I will remember that outside you are 'One-Five'."

As she said the number Vale turned his head towards the door as if instinctively he was afraid of being overheard.

Then he said:

"I wonder if you would give me something to drink? It seems absurd, but because I am sitting up I feel giddy."

"That is because you still have a temperature," Novella said.

There was a jug on the table with a glass beside it, and Novella guessed it contained barley water.

It was what Nanny had always given to her when she was ill.

She half-filled the glass and carried it to Vale.

He drank it down quickly, then started to write.

Because she did not wish to appear to be prying, Novella stood at the window looking out into the garden.

It looked very peaceful.

The birds were singing in the trees.

The daffodils were coming into bloom, and the lilac and syringa bushes were in bud.

The war and everything appertaining to it seemed far away.

Because the fighting had gone on for so many years it was not so vividly omnipresent as it had been when it first started except for Mothers and wives like her Mother.

Yet now in the peace and tranquillity of the countryside where nothing ever happened a man had been wounded fighting against those who wished to kill him.

And because he was unable to go himself, she was to take a secret letter to the Minister for War.

'It cannot be true' she thought. 'I must be dreaming all this!'

She looked back as if to make sure that the Stranger was there in bed, and he said:

"I have finished."

Novella walked towards him.

He was folding the paper on which he had been writing into a small square.

"I want you to carry this somewhere on your body" he said, "until you can give it to the man to whom I am sending you. You must promise me that it will be with you both by day and by night. If by any chance you cannot proceed any further or feel menaced by someone unknown, you will destroy it."

He spoke so seriously that Novella was aware of the importance of the paper he held out to her.

She took it from him and stood for a moment looking down at the small folded piece of paper.

Almost as if he compelled her to do so, she slipped it into her gown so that it lay against her skin between her breasts.

Vale had not suggested it; had not said a word.

Yet she had known that was exactly what he wanted.

"Thank you!" he said quietly.

Then as if the effort had been too much for him he slipped down in the bed and his head was against the pillow.

Novella moved the writing-paper and pen and ink and put them on top of the chest-of-drawers.

She added the blotter then turned back to the bed to speak to Vale.

He was fast asleep.

. . . . . . .

After lunching alone, Novella ordered the pony-cart which she always drove herself.

She went off to the village of Little Bedlington to see Miss Graham.

It was very like their own village, only smaller.

The cottages had only recently been re-thatched.

Miss Graham lived in one of the prettiest of the cottages with the largest garden.

She was in fact picking primroses when Novella stopped outside the gate.

She was a woman of nearly sixty who had retired because there was no need for her to go on working.

She had a small pension from Novella's Father.

She had also been left a few hundred pounds a year when her own Father died.

Always very neat and tidy, there was not a hair out of place on her grey head.

Now she turned to see who was stopping outside.

"Novella!" she exclaimed. "I was not expecting to see you!"

Novella climbed out of the pony-cart.

She left the pony who was old and rather lazy to crop the grass at the side of the road.

She knew he would not wander far.

She kissed her old Governess saying:

"I thought you would be surprised to see me, but I have come to beg a favour."

"Of course, my dear," Miss Graham said. "You know I will be only too delighted. Come inside and I will make you a cup of tea or coffee, if you prefer?"

"Coffee, please," Novella said. "I cannot stay long, but I have come to ask you if you would come with me to London tomorrow morning."

"To London?" Miss Graham exclaimed.

She sounded so surprised that Novella laughed.

"I thought it would be something you would not expect," she said, "but I have to go to London on business which concerns Papa."

"Then of course I will come with you," Miss Graham said. "How long do you think it will take us?"

"Two days to get there, and we will stay at the same Posting Inns where Papa always used to stay when I was with him," Novella said. "And there will be no need for us to stay more than one night in London."

She paused before she said a little anxiously:

"You are quite certain it will not be too much for you?"

"Certainly not!" Miss Graham said quickly. "I may be growing old, but I am not yet senile! It will be something new which I shall enjoy."

She gave a little laugh before she added:

"I do not mind telling you, Novella, that I sometimes find time hanging heavily on my hands, with nobody to teach and no naughty child to correct."

Novella laughed.

"I can see I have been very stupid not to have asked you to help me before."

"You mean you have wanted to?" Miss Graham asked somewhat pathetically.

"Of course I have wanted to," Novella said, "but I thought you were enjoying a rest."

46

"As I have just said, I may be getting old, but I am still too young to be doing nothing," Miss Graham replied.

"Then when we come back," Novella said, "you must come to the Hall and help me with Mama. Things have been very difficult lately."

"How is your Mother?" Miss Graham asked. "I am so sorry she is not yet better."

"I think it is more mental than physical," Novella replied. "She misses Papa so much. I am sure she needs somebody to read to her and talk to her about old times. It would stop her from brooding alone, as she does at the moment."

"How can you have been so foolish as not to have told me all this sooner?" Miss Graham asked.

Novella recognised the tone of voice she used when she thought something was stupid or wrong.

"I am sorry," she said quickly, "and the moment we get back from London you must come and stay. I promise that very soon you will be complaining that you never have a minute to yourself."

"That is exactly what I want," Miss Graham replied. She always liked to have the last word.

. . . . . . .

As the Chaise in which Novella was to journey was just coming round to the front door she went to Vale's bedroom.

Nanny had already given him his breakfast and Dawkins had shaved him.

He was therefore looking, Novella thought, much better than he had before.

But Nanny said he still had a temperature and on no account should he get out of bed.

Novella came beside him.

She was looking extremely beautiful in her close-fitting blue coat with a very pretty bonnet trimmed with flowers.

He looked at her for some moments without speaking.

"You will be all right while I am away," Novella said.

"It is you I am worrying about," Vale replied. "I have been cursing myself for being so weak and helpless. I know I have no right to ask you to do something like this."

"You have every right to do so," Novella said, "if it concerns men like Papa, who are fighting against that monster Bonaparte."

"It is something no woman should do," Vale said, "and if I were half the man I should be, nothing would prevent me from going to London."

"Now you are being stupid," Novella said. "I shall be quite all right. Miss Graham will look after me, and Nanny will look after you."

She paused before she said:

"And when I come back .. perhaps you will tell me .. a tiny bit more about .. this mystery."

Vale put out his right hand.

"I know I am making you curious," he said, "but I am deliberately keeping you in the dark just in case, although it is a very outside chance, someone tries to force you to tell them all you know."

Novella had her hand in his and now her fingers tightened.

"Y .. you mean .. someone might .. kidnap me?" she faltered.

"Not as bad as that," Vale said, "but you might

be intimidated, which can, I assure you, in certain circumstances be very unpleasant."

Novella gave a little shiver.

At the same time she said:

"I am . . sure I will be . . all right."

"I am praying you will be," Vale said, "and once again Novella, I can only say thank you. I know of no other woman who would be as courageous as you are being."

To Novella's surprise, he drew her hand towards him and touched it with his lips.

"When you come back," he said, "I will no longer keep you in ignorance, and I will tell you once again how very wonderful you are."

His voice was very deep and Novella blushed.

Then as she walked towards the door she said:

"Take care of yourself, and Dawkins has strict instructions to admit nobody to the house. Nanny will guard you like a dragon, and I assure you, she can be very fierce, if she wishes to be!"

Vale gave a little laugh.

"I have learnt that already!" he said. "So come back as quickly as you can."

"I promise to do that," Novella answered.

He smiled at her, but she thought his eyes looked worried.

As she ran down the stairs she wished she knew a little more about the reason for the journey to London.

She thought it seemed absurd to drive so far just to deliver a small piece of paper to one particular man.

Then she remembered that she might be saving the lives of men like her Father who were fighting against overwhelming odds.

'When it is all over, Papa will come home,' she thought, 'and then everything will be different.'

Miss Graham was waiting for her in the hall.

"Come along, Novella!" she said as if she was still in the School-Room. "The sooner we can get away, the sooner we can come home."

"Yes, of course, Miss Graham," Novella said obediently.

Hurrying down the steps, they got into the Chaise and set off.

# CHAPTER THREE

Novella and Miss Graham stayed the night at a comfortable Posting Inn which they reached before dinner-time.

The horses were tired, but were still going well.

Novella put them in charge of an ostler who remembered her Father.

The proprietor was delighted to see her again.

A maid in a mob-cap escorted Novella and Miss Graham upstairs to the first floor.

There was a long corridor with small bedrooms opening out of it.

The first room, which was slightly larger Novella insisted on Miss Graham having.

The maid took her into the one next door.

There was nothing unusual about it and she washed and changed into one of the simple gowns she wore at home.

Miss Graham was ready at the same time as she was and they went down together to the Dining-Room.

It was a square and rather ugly room with chairs covered in dark green leather.

The waiter took them to a table in the window and recommended various things on the menu.

The food when it came was edible but not particularly exciting.

However after the long ride Novella was tired and looking forward to going to bed early.

There were about eight other people in the room who were obviously staying in the Hotel.

Another small party arrived when they were half-way through dinner.

Just as they were finishing the last course, a man came in alone.

Novella did not know why but the moment she looked up quite casually and saw him enter the room she felt alert.

He was quite ordinary looking, not particularly well-dressed.

He might have been a commercial traveller, but was certainly not a gentleman.

As he sat down at a table some distance from theirs she had a strange feeling he was looking at her.

She could not explain it herself but she was intensely aware that his eyes were on her.

She suddenly felt afraid.

She was conscious of the note which Vale had given her lying between her breasts.

At the same time she was sensible enough to tell herself it was no use being frightened by shadows.

Or for that matter by strangers.

The waiter had suggested they should have coffee in the sitting-room and they agreed.

As it happened neither Miss Graham nor Novella liked coffee last thing at night but Miss Graham enjoyed a cup of tea.

They sat down near the fireplace in what was

quite a comfortable room from a Posting Inn's point of view.

Novella said she would also like a cup of very weak tea.

"I'll bring it at once Miss," the waiter said.

It took a little longer than if they had asked for coffee which was ready for the other guests.

Having drunk their tea, Novella said:

"If you are not tired Miss Graham, I am."

"You drove so well today," Miss Graham replied "and I am sure your Father would be proud of you."

"He was always very insistent that I should ride well if you remember, from the time I was about ten years of age."

"I think you were only nine," Miss Graham said. "But he was very firm with you and sometimes I thought he asked too much of a child."

Novella laughed.

"Well you can see the result now I am grown up."

"I am actually very impressed," Miss Graham said, "and I am sure it will not take us long to get to London."

"We will not try to challenge the King's record when he was Prince Regent and drove from London to Brighton in one day and in record time," Novella said.

"I remember that," Miss Graham said, "and everyone was tremendously impressed at the time. I think, although it would upset him, that his record has been beaten since."

"The roads have improved a great deal recently," Novella remarked.

"That is true," Miss Graham agreed.

They finished their tea and went slowly upstairs.

Novella went into Miss Graham's room to see she had everything she wanted and then kissed her goodnight.

"I am so grateful to you for coming with me, it is lovely to have you."

"I am enjoying myself more than I have for a long time," Miss Graham answered, "and if anyone is grateful it is me."

Novella laughed.

"Well at least so far, so good and we had better be off early tomorrow morning."

"Yes, of course," Miss Graham said.

Novella went to her own room.

As she did so she saw that the maid had left two candles on the dressing table and a third one by the bed.

As she shut the door she suddenly had the strangest feeling that the room had been searched.

She could not think why it came into her mind.

Yet it may have been that her dressing gown had been moved from where she put it on the chair.

When she reached the dressing table she was almost sure her brush and comb and other things she had laid out had been touched.

She opened the drawers.

She had only put a few things inside them.

Although it seemed absurd she was sure they had been turned over and someone had looked underneath them.

Then she remembered the man downstairs.

With a little shudder she thought he might have been sent by Lord Grimstone to watch her.

It was certainly likely if His Lordship was aware she was going to London.

He would think unless he could prove otherwise that she was carrying information from the man she was hiding.

Novella put her hands up to her forehead.

"I am making all this up" she said, "I cannot have been watched. I must be dreaming."

On impulse she crossed the room.

When she looked at the door she was aware that the key was not there.

She was almost certain, although she could not have sworn to it in a Court of Law, that the key had been in the lock when she had gone downstairs to dinner.

She had not locked her door because she knew the maid would come in and arrange the bed before she returned.

Also the curtains had not been drawn over the window.

If that had been done that would account for one person coming into the room.

But the maid would not have taken away the key.

Also as she was young and countrified, she would not have been feeling about in a guest's drawers.

Yet there was every reason if Lord Grimstone was suspicious that his spy, if that was who the man was, should do so.

Novella looked around the room and wondered what she should do.

It was difficult to move the furniture which consisted of a dressing table and chest-of-drawers in front of the door.

She was suddenly frightened lest the man should come into the room when she was asleep.

He might force her to tell him if she carried any information of importance.

She might lie, but he could torture her to tell the truth.

Then it might be impossible not to give him the secret piece of paper she held between her breasts.

She was getting more and more frightened and she thought wildly she must do something.

The obvious thing would be to go to Miss Graham and say she wanted to stay in her room.

She could sleep on the floor if necessary.

Then she remembered that Vale had trusted her not to tell anyone, and that included Miss Graham, what she was carrying for Viscount Palmerston.

'I have got to do something,' she told herself. 'I cannot stay here and wait for that man to come in through the door.'

She tried to think clearly as her Father would have told her to.

She had to control the fear which was rising until she wanted to scream!

It was almost impossible.

'As Papa's daughter I must be brave' she thought 'and think what he would advise me to do. If only I could tell him how frightened I am.'

She shut her eyes for a moment and sent up a little prayer.

"Please . . God help me . . please," she breathed.

Then almost as if there was an answer from Heaven itself, she knew the answer.

She picked up her nightgown, her dressing gown and her slippers.

Carrying the candle which was by the bed she went out into the corridor.

The room opposite hers and the one next door were both occupied by guests.

She knew this because outside one door was a pair of men's shoes.

Outside the other were a man's and a lady's pair waiting for the boot-boy to clean them.

She went a little further down the corridor.

She listened at a door which had nothing outside it.

Then rather nervously in case she was intruding on someone she opened the door.

The room was in darkness and when she lifted her candle she could see it was unoccupied.

She slipped in and shut the door behind her.

As she expected there was a key and she locked herself in.

The room was almost the same as the one she had left.

The only difference was the curtains had not been pulled and the bed had not been turned down.

She pulled the curtains and then undressed slowly.

When she took off her gown she took the piece of paper Vale had given her and put it down on the dressing table.

Then she asked herself what she should say if the man who was spying on her for Lord Grimstone forced his way into the room.

He would ask her if she was hiding anything.

If she was only wearing her nightgown it would be obvious if she carried the note in the same way as in the daytime.

If she said no, he might also search the room.

He would expect her, being a woman, to hide things in obvious places.

Like under her pillow, under a piece of china, or perhaps beneath the homemade pin cushion which stood on the dressing table.

Then she remembered a story she had read once.

How some very important documents had been hidden under the corner of a carpet where no one had thought to look for them.

Wrapping Vale's note in her handkerchief she slipped it under the carpet.

She thought as she did how terrible it would be if in the morning she left it behind.

There was of course no chance of that.

Every nerve in her body was alert in case the man she had seen downstairs should try to find her in this new room.

Finally because she knew she had a long day in front of her tomorrow and she was in fact very tired, she got into bed.

At first she lay stiffly listening to hear if anyone came into the corridor.

About half an hour passed before the married couple who were sleeping opposite came upstairs.

They were laughing and talking as they went into their bedroom.

Novella felt they had perhaps dined well.

There were sounds coming from the room for some time after they had entered it.

Then there was silence.

She had fallen asleep when suddenly she awoke with a start.

There seemed no reason for her to wake and yet she was aware her whole body was tense.

She raised her head from the pillow so that she could hear more clearly.

It was then she heard a door shut quietly.

She was almost certain it was the door of the room she had left.

This meant, when he thought everyone else was asleep, Lord Grimstone's spy had come upstairs.

He intended to force her to give him what he wanted.

Perhaps it was just her imagination!

At the same time she was sure she was right in thinking that he was, at this moment, inside her room.

She was convinced this was true when a moment later she heard the door open again.

Then she sat up and instinctively put her hands over her lips in case she should scream.

Someone was walking very slowly and heavily as a man would do, down the corridor towards the room where she was now.

His footsteps were very quiet and yet she could hear them.

Now the man had stopped outside her door.

She knew he was looking for her because she was not in the bedroom in which she had undressed before dinner.

The footsteps stopped and she thought she could hear breathing.

She knew he was listening to see if there was anyone inside the room.

Because she was so frightened she was trembling all over.

But she still held her fingers to her lips just in case she should make a sound.

She waited which seemed for a very long time before he turned the handle in the door.

It was then with the greatest difficulty that Novella kept silent.

She wanted to scream and scream so that everyone who was near would come to see what was happening.

Then she realised that because she had locked the door the man outside could not open it.

She knew she was safe and he could not reach her.

For a long time he stood there.

Now she was convinced she could hear him breathing as if he was annoyed.

Also as if he had no idea how, because the door was locked, he could reach her.

Then when she felt she would almost faint because the tension was so intense she heard him turn.

He was moving very slowly back the way he had come.

She thought perhaps he might go into her original room and have another look.

But he went on to the end of the corridor and downstairs.

It was only when she could no longer hear his footsteps or even imagine she could hear them, that she gave a deep sigh.

It seemed to come from the very depths of her body.

She lay down on the pillow.

She had outwitted him and at the same time she was well aware that she was being watched.

There was no question that Lord Grimstone had not been told she had gone to London.

He also suspected she might be carrying information that could be held against him.

Novella had been so afraid of what had happened and because it had taken so long she found now she was shivering with the cold.

She pulled the sheets and blankets over her and cuddled down in the bed.

The man had gone away, there was nothing further he could do apart from breaking down the door and attracting attention.

"Thank You God .. thank You," she said fervently.

Although she felt she was safe it was still a long time before she could fall asleep.

. . . . . . .

Novella rose early next morning and moved back into the room she was supposed to occupy.

She was careful to remember to take Vale's note with her.

She hoped no one would be aware that she had slept in a different room to what was expected.

She tidied the bed and spread the cover over it.

She pulled back the curtains.

She dressed in the room she had been in originally.

She thought as she did so there was no reason for anyone to know she had spent the night elsewhere.

The only person to have been suspicious would have been of course Lord Grimstone's spy.

She wondered rather nervously if he would

follow her and Miss Graham to their next Posting Inn.

Perhaps he would expect them to go straight on to London.

Seeing where her home was and driving to London, it had not been difficult for anyone to guess they would stay at the 'Cock and Feathers.'

It was the best known of the Posting Inns on the London Road and patronised by nearly everyone who lived in the Hythe area.

The next Inn was definitely more problematic.

As they approached it late in the evening they were still some miles from London.

Novella thought they would be sensible to rest there for the night.

The horses from the 'Cock and Feathers' were not as good as their own and did not travel as fast.

However they had been driven by their groom which had saved Novella from having to drive.

When she asked them they strongly recommended the 'Green Dragon' to any of the other Inns on the road.

It was where her Father had stayed.

If Lord Grimstone used Posting Inns, Novella thought he would stay there too.

There was however no point in being uncomfortable.

If the spy was determined to find her he only had to go from one Inn to another until he did so.

Perhaps he had given up the chase!

But thinking that did not prevent Novella from, several times during the day, looking back to see if she was being followed.

"You seem a little worried dear," Miss Graham said as they neared the *'Green Dragon.'* "I hope this rush to London will not be too much for you."

"No, of course not," Novella said. "I was just wondering how much longer we will take but I think we would be just as comfortable staying here as in London."

"If you ask my opinion," Miss Graham said, "I think you have done enough for one day. Quite frankly I am looking forward to my bed."

"Then the vote is definitely for the *'Green Dragon'*!" Novella smiled.

They turned into the large courtyard.

When the Proprietor heard Novella's name he asked after her Father.

"Papa is of course fighting with Wellington's Army," Novella answered.

"God Bless him and I hopes he comes back to you soon," the Proprietor said.

"That is what we want and perhaps this wicked war will end sooner than we expect," Novella answered.

"Wicked's the right word for it," the Proprietor agreed. "The missus be worried stiff about our eldest boy and we 'ave had no news about th' younger for over six months 'cos he be in the Navy."

"I do hope you hear soon," Novella said.

As the maid showed her and Miss Graham up to their rooms, she thought:

'There is no one in the whole country who is not affected in one way or another by the beastly war.'

"How can it go on for so long?" she asked as many people had asked before her.

Yet as the years passed there seemed no end to it.

The rooms she had been shown were very much like the ones they had slept in the night before.

The maid said:

"You are lucky to get these Miss, we have been busy today and they be the only ones left that is not taken."

"We are certainly very lucky," Novella replied.

The moment she went into her own room she took the key out of the lock and put it into her handbag.

She was not going to be caught as she had been last night if by any chance the spy was following her.

She changed from her travelling gown into the same one she had worn last night for dinner.

As she did so she told herself:

'Perhaps the whole thing is a lot of nonsense.'

Would Lord Grimstone really go to such lengths as to send a spy following her all the way to London?

She had told everyone she had to go on her Father's business, what would he gain if he went back empty-handed?

'I must be very careful' she thought, 'but at the same time I cannot believe this is really happening!'

When Miss Graham was ready they went down to dinner early.

"I must confess to being a little stiff," Miss Graham said, "I think the truth is the Chaise we were driving in today is not as comfortable as your own."

"I thought the same," Novella agreed. "Papa

always said however it was a mistake to use our own vehicle because if they handled it badly and the horses were not accustomed to it, it was our fault rather than theirs."

"I am sure your Father is right," Miss Graham said, "but at the same time I shall be glad when you are driving again and there is more room for us both."

They were talking casually as they entered the Dining-Room.

Then as the head waiter guided them to a table, Novella saw '*him*' there waiting for her.

He had an unpleasant twist to his lips.

She felt her heart give a startled jump.

Then as she sat down she forced herself to look at the spy who was only two tables away.

He was certainly an unpleasant individual.

He was about 40 years of age and there was, she thought, something hard and cruel about his eyes.

Also in the thinness of his lips.

Because she was staring at him he was staring back.

She had the uncomfortable feeling he knew where she was carrying the precious note that Vale had given her.

The dinner was not as good as it had been the previous evening.

The pastry on the tart was not very well cooked.

Miss Graham pushed it on one side.

"It is really not worth eating," she said, "and as I am tired, I think Novella dear we should go to bed. You will want to be in good form tomorrow if you have to do any business on behalf of your Father."

"Yes of course," Novella agreed.

She rose to her feet, conscious that the man opposite her was watching every movement.

As they went up the oak stairs which were not covered by a carpet, she wondered what she should do.

She could lock herself in as she had last night.

But she had a feeling that because he seemed so sure of himself, he had some idea of how he could reach her.

They reached Miss Graham's room which was in fact exactly the same as the one next door, suddenly Novella said:

"I wonder if you will think it very odd of me if I ask if I can sleep in your room."

Miss Graham looked surprised.

"Why do you ask that?" she said.

"I know you will laugh at me," Novella said, "but I have a feeling mine is haunted and I know you do not believe in such things."

"Certainly not," Miss Graham said sharply. "As I have told you over and over again ever since you were a small child there are no such things as ghosts, they are just a part of a person's imagination."

Novella managed to give a little chuckle.

"You told me that when I thought I saw a ghost in the Library and also one in the Hall."

Miss Graham laughed.

"I remember quite well the latter. It was actually one of the footmen who had drunk too much and had fallen down behind the table on which the hats were laid out. When you heard him snoring you came running into my room saying the ghost in the Hall was going to eat you up."

"I was only five at the time," Novella replied, "and he did make very strange noises."

"What makes you think there is a ghost in the room tonight?"

"I do not know," she said. "I have just got a squiggle in my spine and my hair feels as if it is rising up on my head."

"If you ask me it is just tiredness," Miss Graham said. "But of course you sleep here my dear. If the ghost wakes me in the middle of the night I will give it a piece of my mind."

"Now you are making me feel I am being foolish," Novella said. "But thank you very much for being so kind."

She kissed Miss Graham.

Then she went into the room to bring out her own things and helped Miss Graham to carry hers next door.

When she had made sure she had left nothing behind she kissed Miss Graham again and said:

"You are very kind to me and it is lovely to think that just like the old days you are looking after me."

"That is exactly what I intend to do," Miss Graham said, "now go to bed and no more talking."

She was laughing as she shut her door.

Novella did the same, turning the key in the lock.

Then she undressed quickly and got into bed.

She was in fact so tired that she fell asleep at once.

When she awoke it was morning and the sun was coming in through the side of the curtains.

She looked at the clock she had with her and found it was 7 o'clock.

Then as she did so there was a knock on the door.

She got out of bed to open it.

The maid came in with some hot water with which to wash and also a cup of tea and a thin slice of bread and butter.

"It's a nice morning Miss, an' breakfast 'll be ready as soon as you wants it."

"Thank you very much," Novella said.

She had just finished dressing when Miss Graham came into her room.

"Are you ready dear?" she asked.

"I only have to put my hat on," Novella replied.

"I do hope you slept well. It was a good thing you were not with me," Miss Graham said, "or you would have thought you were seeing ghosts."

"Why, what happened?" Novella asked.

"Well actually I was fast asleep," Miss Graham replied, "when suddenly I was woken by the sound of something falling on the floor."

Novella was holding her breath.

Her eyes were on Miss Graham as she went on:

"The next moment the door opened and a man came in."

"A man?" Novella exclaimed, knowing as she spoke who it was.

"Yes, a strange man, a man who I think I saw downstairs when we were having dinner," Miss Graham answered. "He was carrying a candle in his hand and when he saw me looking at him, he stared at me in astonishment and then he said:

" 'Sorry! I must have come to the wrong room.'

" 'You certainly have'," I replied. "But even as

he spoke he went out and shut the door quite sharply."

Novella did not say anything and after a moment Miss Graham went on:

"The strange thing was, lying on the floor was the key he must have pushed out of the lock while he used another key to let himself in. I call it extremely careless of this Inn to have two keys for the same door."

"It does seem strange," Novella answered.

At the same time she was thanking God she had been wise enough to change rooms with Miss Graham.

Once again Vale's special letter for the Secretary of State for War was safe.

As there was nothing she could say, Novella merely fastened her luggage.

She realised as she moved towards the door Miss Graham was waiting for her.

"They can be putting the luggage in the Chaise while we have breakfast," Novella said, "and we will be wise to get into London before the traffic increases as it always does later in the morning."

Miss Graham agreed.

As they went down the stairs Novella was thinking she had been very lucky as well as clever in being able to outwit Lord Grimstone's spy.

She thought perhaps they would see him in the Dining-Room.

Either he had left earlier or was sleeping late because there was no sign of him.

Miss Graham was in good spirits.

She kept saying it was such a change from the long days she had spent with no one to talk to, and nothing to do.

"Never again," she said to Novella, "will I sit about with idle hands, and I am looking forward to being with your Mother."

"I know Mama would love to have you," Novella said.

Miss Graham had been very discreet.

She did not ask her why she was going to London after she had said it was on her Father's business.

Novella was wondering what she should say when she drove the Chaise down Whitehall.

As she stopped outside The War Office she was sure Miss Graham would not ask her any awkward questions.

Before Novella could suggest it, she said:

"I will stay in the Chaise, dear, I am sure you do not want me to come in with you."

"I will try not to be long," Novella answered.

She was looking very pretty as she stepped out in the Spring sunshine.

She was wearing the same blue coat and pretty bonnet in which she had left home.

As she walked up the steps and in through the imposing entrance, Miss Graham gave a sigh.

The war had prevented Novella, like so many other girls, from having a Season in London.

There would have been a Ball given for her.

She would have been invited to a great number of other Balls and entertainments with débutantes of the same age.

Novella was feeling very nervous.

She was afraid that what Vale had given her was of no importance. If so she had made the journey for nothing.

Then she remembered how, despite his wound, he had seemed authoritative and sure of himself.

That reassured her that the little piece of paper he had given her was something the Secretary of State for War would be glad to have.

This was the Viscount Palmerston of whom her Father had often spoken.

Therefore when she was approached by a man in uniform she said:

"I wish please to see the Secretary of State for War, Viscount Palmerston."

"Will you tell me your name, Ma'am?"

"Will you inform His Lordship it is Miss Novella Wentmore who is the daughter of General Sir Alexander Wentmore."

She thought her Father's name brought an expression of recognition into the face of the soldier questioning her.

Having offered her a chair, he hurried away.

It was in fact not many minutes before she was ushered into the presence of the Viscount Palmerston.

He was exceedingly good-looking and had a gracious air about him which made him very attractive to women.

He was the most able and powerful Secretary For War Britain had ever had.

Despite being chiefly known as a 'Man of Fashion' he was an efficient and devoted Administrator.

He greeted Novella with a smile which she found as irresistible as a large number of beautiful Ladies had before her.

"I am delighted to meet you, Miss Wentmore," the Viscount said, "and I have heard good news of your Father recently, whose capabilities are very much appreciated by the Duke of Wellington."

Novella flushed with pleasure at hearing her Father spoken of so warmly, and the Viscount asked:

"Will you sit down, Miss Wentmore, and tell me why you are here?"

After a glance round to be sure they were alone, Novella handed to him the piece of paper Vale had given her.

"I have brought this to you My Lord," she said, "from 'One-Five.'"

The Viscount stiffened and looked at her in astonishment.

Then he said as if he could hardly believe his ears:

"Did you say it was from One-Five?"

"Yes, My Lord."

The Viscount stared at her.

Then without asking any more questions he opened the piece of writing-paper.

As he did so he rose to his feet.

He sat down again and opened a drawer with a key which he took from his waist-coat pocket.

He drew out a small blue book.

As he set it down on his blotter Novella guessed he was using it to decipher a code.

The Viscount studied the book and the paper for quite a long time before he said:

"What you have brought me, Miss Wentmore, is extremely interesting and important, and I feel sure you have spoken of it to no one."

"No one, My Lord. I was told to keep it completely secret."

"And you know where One-Five is?"

"Yes, My Lord."

"Will you tell me where?"

"He is at my home, Wentmore Hall at Hythe."

The Viscount gave a deep sigh.

Novella was not sure, but she thought it was one of relief.

Then he said:

"I am not going to ask you any unnecessary questions, but can you tell me why he is there?"

"Yes My Lord," Novella answered, "and I feel sure it is right for you to know that he is in hiding."

"In hiding?" the Viscount questioned in astonishment. "From whom?"

For a moment Novella hesitated.

Then she decided it was best to tell him the whole truth.

"One-Five," she said, "came running into my house three days ago. He begged me to save him because some men were trying to kill him."

The Viscount's eyes widened, but he did not speak and she went on:

"He had been shot in the arm and the blood was pouring over his hand. Because I believed him, I hid him."

She thought the Viscount would ask her where, but when he said nothing she went on:

"He was only just out of sight when Lord Grimstone arrived."

"Lord Grimstone?" the Viscount questioned.

"Yes, My Lord. He lives a short distance from my home."

"And it was Grimstone who wanted to kill One-Five. Did he say so?"

"Yes, My Lord. He said he had seen the man he was following enter the house. But when I assured him he was mistaken his men searched the garden, before they left."

"And One-Five is still there?"

"Yes, My Lord. Owing to his wound he developed a high temperature and it was impossible for him to travel to London himself."

"So you came in his place," the Viscount said. "I can only say how exceedingly grateful I am to you."

He looked down again at the paper he held in his hand and said:

"I think you will understand, Miss Wentmore, that I wish to discuss this with the Prime Minister, and I am therefore going to ask you to stay here for a short time. I am sure you would enjoy a cup of coffee, and I will be as quick as I can."

"Thank you My Lord, that would be very nice," Novella replied.

The Viscount rang a bell that stood on his desk and the door opened almost immediately.

"Bring Miss Wentmore coffee," he ordered, "and something to eat with it."

He picked up the piece of paper on his desk, put the little blue book back in its drawer and locked it.

With a warm smile at Novella he left her alone.

Novella looked round the room thinking she had never expected to see the inside of the War Office.

She wondered what her Father would say when he learned about her visit.

She was sure he would say she had done the right thing in saving Vale's life and hiding him from Lord Grimstone.

She was wondering how Lord Grimstone came

into the story, considering that Viscount Palmerston had been so surprised on hearing that he was involved.

"He is a horrible man!" she told herself. "I hope he does not frighten Nanny while I am away."

She had told Dawkins very firmly that no one was to be allowed to enter the house in her absence.

If Lord Grimstone, or anybody else, tried to get in, he was to refuse to open the door to them.

When the coffee arrived, Novella drank it and ate the small pâté sandwiches which were served with it.

She would have been surprised if she had known what a sensation the piece of paper which she had given to Viscount Palmerston was causing.

He had hurriedly driven down Whitehall to No. 10 Downing Street.

As a young man the Prime Minister, now the Earl of Liverpool, had been distinctly handsome, tall, slender and graceful with an engaging air.

But already the cares of Office were beginning to stamp their mark on his face.

His expression actually had hardened.

But his broad forehead and thoughtful gaze revealed to everyone who met him his calm, even character.

Those who worked for him knew he was always logical and fair.

He had made his mark from the moment he entered Parliament, when he had made a remarkably impressive Maiden speech.

Pitt, then Prime Minister, had rated it as "the most able First Speech that had ever been heard from any young Member."

It was described as "full of philosophy and science, strong and perspicuous language, sound and convincing arguments."

The Earl was only thirty years of age when he was made Foreign Secretary soon after the beginning of the War.

It was for any young man an exceptional compliment.

Now he was proving himself over and over again to be a brilliant Administrator.

He was deeply respected by those who worked with him.

When the Viscount was announced, he was alone and rose to his feet saying:

"It is delightful to see you, but somewhat of a surprise."

"I thought that is what it would be," the Viscount answered, "but I have just been brought a note from One-Five, which I think will astonish and delight you."

The Prime Minister's eyes lit up and he said:

"I have been very concerned about One-Five as we had not heard from him."

"So have I," the Viscount agreed, "but he is safe, though wounded, and in hiding in the house of General Sir Alexander Wentmore."

"How on earth did he get there?" the Prime Minister questioned.

"Apparently by the 'skin of his teeth'," the Viscount answered, "but first let me tell you his news."

"That is what I have been waiting for," the Prime Minister said.

"I have decoded his message," the Viscount went on "and it tells us that with the utmost sec-

76

recy and under the pretence of equipping the Spanish Army in Galacia, Wellington is assembling supply ships, guns and ammunition in Corunna for transportation to Santander Bay."

The Prime Minister gave a gasp.

"Santander Bay?" he repeated.

The Viscount smiled.

"Two hundred and fifty miles to the East?"

"I can hardly believe it!" the Prime Minister exclaimed.

"It is true," the Viscount assured him, "and you realise that by doing this he will shorten his communications with England by four hundred land miles, and as many sea miles. Instead of advancing away from his supplies he is moving towards them."

"I can see that," the Prime Minister said. "And with every mile he drives North-East, getting nearer to the sea, from which he draws his strength, his lines of communication will become safer."

"Exactly!" the Viscount agreed. "I cannot remember when the offensive use of sea-power on land has been more clearly envisaged by a soldier."

There was a note of triumph in his voice that made the Prime Minister smile.

Aloud he said:

"You realise that the operation will be attended by difficulties from the Americans?"

"I know that," the Viscount replied.

He did not need to say any more.

Their attack on a defenceless Canadian frontier had indeed been thwarted by a few hundred Regulars under a British Commander-in-Chief.

But both men were aware that American frigates more heavily manned and gunned than their British counterparts, had had three surprise successes at sea.

Then to everybody's astonishment, American Privateers had begun to appear along the Portuguese Coast to prey on Wellington's supply ships.

This was not a serious threat, since the strength of the Royal Navy was immense, and the United States had not even a single capital ship.

But just at this moment it could be tiresome for Wellington if a report on his brilliant new strategy could not safely reach the 'Powers that Be' in London.

"I can understand that Wellington," the Prime Minister was saying, "decided the information we have here was too important to risk it being carried to us by any agent less clever than One-Five."

"That is what I thought," the Viscount agreed, "and now of course we can alert the Navy."

"Which we will do immediately!" the Prime Minister said firmly, "and I can only say thank God that One-Five has reached England."

"Amen to that!" the Viscount said. "I think now we should try to dispose of Grimstone in one way or another."

"I have been thinking that for a long time," the Prime Minister replied, "but, as you well know, we have not enough evidence against him, and I do not wish to 'draw his claws' without learning first who is associating with him."

"All I can think of at the moment," the Viscount said, "is that thanks to Wentmore's extremely pretty daughter, One-Five is alive."

The Prime Minister was silent.

Then after a long pause, he said:

"We both know Grimstone's reputation. Do you think that Wentmore's daughter could help us?"

"She is very young and extremely attractive, and I should think very innocent," the Viscount replied.

The Prime Minister smiled.

"You would certainly be a good judge of that!"

Then as the Viscount did not answer he said in a serious tone:

"Somehow we have to stop this endless drain of gold benefiting Napoleon."

"Very well," the Viscount said, "I will ask her to do what she can, but quite frankly I think we must be satisfied to take Grimstone, on whom we have nearly enough evidence, and forget his accomplices."

"The bullion, and God knows, there is an enormous amount of it" the Prime Minister answered, "is an invaluable source for Napoleon for the purchase of war supplies."

The Viscount held up his hand.

"I know, I know! Very well, I will talk to Miss Wentmore, but it is something I do not like doing."

"Nor do I," the Prime Minister agreed. "At the same time, if we can eliminate Grimstone and his gang, we will be helping Wellington in what I think is the most remarkable and daring strategic plan the British Army has ever undertaken."

The Viscount rose to his feet.

"I agree" he said, "and when One-Five is well enough to come to London we shall learn a great deal more than we know now. For my part, I do not only hope, but I feel it in my bones, that the end is in sight."

"I can only pray you are right," the Prime Minister answered.

As he spoke he put the note the Viscount had given him from One-Five into a locked drawer.

· · · · · · ·

Novella was reading the newspaper that had been brought to her when Viscount Palmerston came back into his office.

She would have got up, but he prevented her from doing so by saying:

"Do not move, Miss Wentmore, I want to talk to you."

She was sitting in a comfortable arm-chair and he sat down in the one next to it.

"First I must tell you," he began, "how pleased and delighted the Prime Minister was with the information you brought us from One-Five. Please tell him on our behalf that it has given us hope and we are deeply grateful that he has managed to reach England."

"I am sure that is what he will want to hear," Novella replied, "and shall I tell him, My Lord, that he must not try to come to meet you himself until he is really well enough to travel?"

The Viscount smiled.

"Tell him that is an order which he must obey!"

Novella thought it was the end of the interview and again would have risen.

However Viscount Palmerston said in a serious tone:

"I have been asked by the Prime Minister, Miss Wentmore, to tell you of the difficulties in which we find ourselves with regard to Lord Grimstone."

"You are asking .. *me* to do .. something?" Novella inquired.

She thought she must have misunderstood what he was saying.

Slowly, as if he was feeling for words, the Viscount said:

"I expect, living by the sea, or near to it, you have heard of the 'Guinea-Boats.' They are the smugglers all along the coast who bring contraband goods to England from France which are paid for in gold."

"Yes .. of course," Novella agreed.

"Well, I was told only last week that the 'Guinea-Boats' are estimated to be carrying back to France ten to twelve thousand guineas *a week* across the Channel."

Novella gasped.

"As much as that? How can it be possible?"

"The golden guinea is the only currency which is acceptable to the French merchants," the Viscount said, "and it is that gold which provides Napoleon with an invaluable source of ready money to buy war supplies from neutral countries."

"The guns which .. kill our soldiers!" Novella said beneath her breath, thinking of her Father.

"Exactly!" the Viscount said. "Napoleon thinks of the English smugglers as his friends and, as I expect you know, the most popular route is the narrow part of the Channel between Boulogne and Dover."

Knowing that was very near to where she lived, Novella drew in a sharp breath.

"I am told," the Viscount went on, "that they achieve such high speeds – as much as nine knots

– they can easily make the return trip in one night."

"Of course, I have . . heard this . . is happening," Novella admitted, "and I have always prayed that none of the men of our village are involved. But as I believe, they can earn as much as a guinea a trip, it is a great temptation to them."

"Of course it is," the Viscount agreed. "So it is their tempter who must be punished – men, for instance, like Lord Grimstone – who should know better than to betray their own country."

Novella sat up in astonishment.

"Lord Grimstone!" she said. "Do you think he is involved in all this?"

"Very much so," the Viscount replied. "He must have made a fortune for himself from the rich materials he has brought into England and which are sold to stupid women in London who have no idea that they have cost the lives of English soldiers!"

"Then, why . . why," Novella cried, "do . . you not . . arrest Lord Grimstone?"

"That is what I am going to tell you," the Viscount said. "We have reason to believe that he does not work alone, and that quite a number of his friends who are of the same social importance as himself are collaborating with him."

Novella made a little murmur of horror and the Viscount went on.

"They are profiting from the brandy, wine and silks that are smuggled over from France, but we do not know their names. For it is Grimstone who receives the cargoes that come in from Boulogne and other places on the French coast."

Novella was silent.

Then, because she was quick-witted, she asked:
"What are .. you asking .. me to .. do?"

"It seems wrong, I know, but as a soldier's daughter, you will understand that because we are desperate, we feel that, since by a miraculous coincidence Grimstone lives near you and has been to your house, you may be able to find out a little more than we know at the moment."

He spread out his hands in a gesture as he said:

"I promise you, Miss Wentmore, we have tried everything in our power to discover who are in Grimstone's 'gang' as we call them. We have an idea they are in high places and of social importance. We may be wrong, but that is what our instinct tells us. However, we have nothing to go on."

"And .. and you .. are asking .. me," Novella said in a low voice, "to .. to find .. this out for .. you?"

"I am asking you to try," the Viscount answered, "but not to run any risks. Just try if it is possible, and it may not be possible, to discover the names of the gang, or perhaps point us in the direction of where they live so that we can bring these traitors to justice."

"I .. I .. understand," Novella said after a little pause. "I have told you how much I dislike .. Lord Grimstone .. but in fact .. he has .. asked me to .. dine at his house .. and said he wanted to .. see me again."

She hesitated over what she was saying, almost as if the admission was being dragged from her.

"Then all I can beg of you," the Viscount said, "is to accept his invitation to dine with him, properly chaperoned, of course, and when you are in his house to find out anything you can that may give us some indication of how he is operating and with whom he is associating."

Novella was silent.

After a moment the Viscount admitted:

"I know I am asking a lot, but it was the Prime Minister's idea. It seemed to him, as it seems to me, that it was by the mercy of God that One-Five was able to reach you in safety."

"I thought myself that it was . . rather like a miracle," Novella said.

"Then of course," the Viscount smiled, "we are being greedy in asking for another one!'

Novella gave a deep sigh.

"I will . . do my best . . but I am sure it will not be easy . . and Lord Grimstone is . . horrible and makes me creep . . even to talk . . to him!"

"Then do your best to see that he ends up in the Tower of London which is where he belongs!" the Viscount said firmly.

He rose to his feet and as Novella also stood up he said:

"Listen, Miss Wentmore, you are not to take any unnecessary risks and, as I have said, if you dine with Grimstone, make quite certain you are chaperoned."

He paused for a moment as he started to take her hand.

"I think your Father would be very proud of you," he said, "and the Prime Minister and myself thank you for all you have done already."

Because he spoke so quietly and yet sincerely, Novella felt as if the tears were near her eyes.

"I will try . . I promise I will try," she whispered, "but you must not be angry with me if I . . f.fail."

"It would be very difficult for any man to be angry with you, Miss Wentmore, and when I next meet your Father, I will tell him that his daughter is not only very beautiful, but also exceedingly brave!"

He escorted Novella to the door and walked with her to the Chaise that was waiting outside.

He had already looked with approval at Miss Graham.

At the same time, he seemed surprised there was no groom on the carriage.

While Novella was inside the War Office, the horses had been attended to by one of the soldiers on duty.

"So you are driving yourself!" the Viscount exclaimed as she took the reins.

"My Father taught me to drive, as he taught me to ride when I was very small," Novella answered, "but I can assure you, My Lord, this is the most interesting and exciting drive I have ever made."

"I can well believe that!" the Viscount replied. "I hope you will arrive home without mishap."

He stepped back and she smiled at him before she drove away.

When they were out of ear-shot, Miss Graham said:

"I presume that was Viscount Palmerston!"

"Yes, it was," Novella confirmed, "and he said some very nice things about Papa."

"He is an extremely handsome man," Miss Graham observed. "I am not surprised that so many women have been in love with him."

Novella turned her head to look at her in astonishment.

"How do you know that?" she asked.

Miss Graham laughed.

"My dear, everybody talks about men of importance, and if they have a love-affair it is carried on the wind. Everybody knows about it almost before it has begun – or ended!"

Novella laughed.

"I hope that when I have a love-affair, if I ever have one, it will be kept a secret."

"You will have nothing of the sort!" Miss Graham said sharply. "I want to see you married to someone who is as charming, good-looking and clever as your Father. It will be announced in the Court Circulars, and everyone will say what a lucky man he is!"

Novella laughed.

"Now you are making up a Fairy Story! You know that living so quietly in the country as we have since Papa went to war I cannot remember when I last met a young man."

As she spoke, she remembered that she had met Vale.

Yet in such extraordinary circumstances that she still could hardly believe it was true.

It was more like something she had read in a book.

He was certainly handsome, and what was more, very exciting.

She knew now from the way the Viscount had behaved that he was in a Secret Service which no one was allowed to talk about.

As they drove on she was thinking over what Viscount Palmerston had said to her.

She worked it out that Vale must have arrived at Lord Grimstone's house disguised as one of the smugglers.

She had heard that the boats that came from the French coast did not only carry contraband goods which made those who sold them a fortune.

It was whispered they also brought with them French spies.

These men then went to London to obtain information that was useful to Napoleon.

Novella was aware that because the smuggling had become so persistent measures had been taken to stamp it out.

Fishermen were forbidden to build boats with more than six oars.

The Coastguard Service was expanded to prevent cargoes from France being landed.

Wentmore Hall was near the sea.

Novella had therefore always heard people talking about smuggling, not only amongst her Father's friends, but in the village.

Preventive measures on the English coast were naturally being tightened.

As a result the smugglers' galleys which were the quickest means of getting to Calais, were frequently lost.

Crews had been forced to abandon their galleys on the nearest beach.

But the boats were so cheaply and lightly built that their cost of renewal amounted to only a tenth of the profit of a single good run.

Novella had listened to what was said.

But she never, in her wildest dreams, imagined she would become involved with the smugglers. Nor did she expect to learn any more about them than she knew already.

Yet now, to her horror, the Viscount had asked

her to take part in bringing someone as important as Lord Grimstone to justice.

'I . . hate him! I hate . . him!' Novella thought as she drove on.

Then she knew that it was for England's sake, and perhaps too for Vale's.

Therefore she would try to discover what the Viscount wanted to learn even though it meant facing extreme danger.

# CHAPTER FOUR

Novella and Miss Graham stayed the first night at the Posting Inn not far outside London.

They had to return the horses there anyway.

Because they were in a hurry, they set off early the next morning.

After the second night Novella picked up the horses that belonged to her Father.

She was delighted to find they were as fresh and spirited as they usually were.

Because they knew they were going home they moved very much faster than when they were on the way to London.

They turned in at the gates of Wentmore Hall at about six o'clock.

"That was a delightful drive!" Miss Graham exclaimed.

Novella had already asked her if she would prefer to go home first, but she wanted to see Lady Wentmore.

"I feel I have neglected her," Miss Graham said, "I was so afraid of pushing myself forward and being a bore."

"You could never be that!" Novella said sincerely.

Miss Graham smiled.

"I know what a boring lot Governesses, Tutors and Nannies can be when they start talking about the 'old days!' "

Novella laughed.

"Well, that is something I want to talk to you about, and I know Mama does too, so we can all sit down together and enjoy ourselves."

As she spoke she wondered if she would have the time. Perhaps her new duties would prevent her from being so much with her Mother.

One thing she was determined, she would not tell her Mother what she had been asked to do when she was in London.

She was quite sure her Mother would be horrified at the idea and would prevent her from having anything to do with Lord Grimstone.

"Papa will understand," Novella told herself.

Everybody had been upset by the war and the difficulties it had caused.

Most of all the country was suffering from a great deal of poverty.

This was despite the fact that the farmers had been able to sell all their crops at good prices, as everyone, including the Army under Wellington, required food.

"It must be over soon!" Novella said to herself.

She knew that if there was anything she could do to bring peace nearer, she must do it, however frightening it might be.

Wentmore Hall looked very beautiful as they drove up the drive.

The sun was shining on its diamond-paned windows.

They drew up outside the front door and the old groom came hurrying from the stables.

Only then did Novella remember she had not told Miss Graham they had a visitor.

She thought however she would be wise to consult first with Vale as to what he wanted her to say.

He had been so secretive about himself.

Also the manner in which Viscount Palmerston had spoken of him made Novella aware that she had to be very careful in everything she said.

Old Abbey was asking her how the horses had behaved.

"They were perfect!" Novella said. "And we have come home at what I am sure has been a record speed."

The old man took the compliment to himself.

After Novella and Miss Graham had stepped out of the Chaise, he drove it away to the stable-yard.

Dawkins came to greet her in the hall.

Then Novella ran upstairs, with Miss Graham following her.

When she went into her Mother's room, Lady Wentmore held out her arms.

"Darling, you are back!" she said. "I have been so worried about you."

"I was afraid you might be, Mama," Novella said, "but here I am, safe and sound, and I have brought you a guest."

As she spoke she thought it was a silly thing to say in case her Mother should exclaim: "Another one?"

But as Miss Graham appeared in the doorway Lady Wentmore gave a little cry of delight.

"How delightful to see you!" she exclaimed. "I

have been wondering how you are, and if you are happy in the village."

"It has made me much happier to have an invitation from Novella to stay here," Miss Graham said, "and help her to look after you."

"That is a splendid idea!" Lady Wentmore said. "In fact I am feeling happier, because not only has Novella come back, but I have also had a letter from her Father!"

"A letter from Papa?" Novella cried. "Oh Mama, how exciting! What does he say?"

"Very little about what he is doing," Lady Wentmore replied, "but he is missing us, and hoping to see us all again very soon."

After she had spoken she paused, then said in a low voice:

"Do you really think he means that there is a chance of his coming home soon?"

"I am sure there is Mama," Novella said. "The war cannot last forever, and when Papa is home again it will just seem like a bad dream."

Lady Wentmore sighed.

"It has been so long, so very long, that I am almost afraid it will never end."

She was speaking as if to herself and Novella said quickly:

"Of course it is going to end, and I am sure Papa is being prophetic when he says he will see us soon."

Lady Wentmore did not answer and Novella went on:

"I will go and take off my bonnet and cloak which are covered in dust, and I am sure, Miss Graham, you would like to do the same."

"I would like first to talk to your Mother," Miss

Graham said and sat down in the chair nearest the bed.

Novella went outside into the passage and saw Nanny coming towards her from the Servants' quarters.

She ran towards her saying:

"I am back, Nanny! What has been happening while I have been away?"

Nanny opened the door of one of the unoccupied bedrooms and drew her inside.

"I've quite a lot to tell you, Miss Novella" she said, "but I hear that you've brought Miss Graham back with you and it's best for her to know nothing."

"Yes, of course," Novella agreed, "but what has happened?"

"Mr. Vale's better – I can say that!" Nanny said. "But he's not yet well enough to go gallivanting about or he'll have his wound bleeding again."

"I am sure you can prevent him from doing anything foolish," Novella said.

"I can try," Nanny answered, "but he's a will of his own, has that one!"

Novella gave a little laugh and Nanny went on:

"I understand he has to be very careful. That Lord what's-his-name's been sneaking about the place, and though no one's said anything, he's got his suspicions that Mr. Vale's here."

"Oh, Nanny, he must not find him," Novella cried.

"He's not come inside the house," Nanny replied. "Mr. Dawkins 'as seen to that, and so have I. But I wouldn't trust him, not for half-a-second!"

"Nor would I," Novella agreed.

She knew Nanny would not have said this unless she was really worried, and she said quickly:

"I will go and take off my bonnet and wash the dust away. Then I would like to see Mr. Vale."

"He's waiting to see you," Nanny said, "and whatever you're bringing him from London, I hope it's good news."

Novella did not answer.

As she went to her bedroom she thought that as far as Vale was concerned the news might be good.

But for her personally it was definitely bad.

When she went in to see Vale ten minutes later it was to find him not in bed, but sitting in the window.

He was not dressed, but was wearing a long dark robe.

It had belonged to the General and was frogged down the front, giving him a Military appearance.

A white scarf was wound round his neck and he was sitting up in the chair, waiting to greet her.

She thought how handsome he looked.

And above all so much better in health than when she had last seen him.

His left arm was in a sling, but he held out his right hand in greeting.

As she took it, she felt his fingers close almost fiercely over hers.

"You are back!" he exclaimed. "I feel as if you have been away for a hundred years!"

"Not quite as long as that!" Novella smiled. "But I have a lot to tell you."

"You know I want to hear it," Vale answered.

She sat down in the chair opposite his and

started her story from the moment she walked into the Ministry of War.

"I felt a little nervous," she admitted, "but once I had met Viscount Palmerston, I found him charming."

"There has never been a woman who did not," Vale remarked.

Novella went on to tell him exactly what happened.

How the Viscount had read the note she had given him and then, she thought, decoded it.

"After that he said he must go and see the Prime Minister," she added.

"That is what I thought he would do," Vale said quietly.

"I waited there for quite a long time," Novella went on, "and when he came back he said how exceedingly grateful he and the Prime Minister were, first that you are alive, and secondly for the information you brought them."

"He did not tell you what it was?" Vale asked.

Novella shook her head.

"No .. but .."

She paused.

"But, what?" Vale prompted.

"He asked me to do something which would .. help the Prime Minister and himself."

Vale looked at her searchingly.

After a moment he asked:

"What is it? I know it is something you do not wish to do."

Hesitatingly, because she felt embarrassed at her own feelings, Novella told him what the Viscount had said about Lord Grimstone.

"I cannot imagine why they do not arrest that man, once and for all!" Vale said angrily.

"That is .. exactly what I .. said," Novella agreed, "but they want first the .. names of those who are .. in league with him – what the Viscount calls his 'Gang'."

There was a moment's silence.

Then Vale said:

"What you are trying to say is that they are asking you to find out the names of these men."

Novella nodded.

"The Viscount said I should .. take no risks .. but as Papa's daughter .. I would know how important it was that .. Napoleon should not go on getting enormous amounts of .. our gold every week to spend on buying the .. weapons to .. kill our soldiers with."

Vale's lips tightened in a hard line.

Then he said:

"You should have refused."

"How .. How .. could I?" Novella asked. "He knows I live only a short way from Lord Grimstone, and His Lordship has already said that he would .. like me to .. dine with him."

"You did not tell me that!"

"There seemed no point in doing so, when I had no intention of accepting such a preposterous invitation."

Vale moved uneasily in his chair.

"I will probably have to kill the man myself!" he said. "But I will not have you involved in this sort of thing!"

"B.but .. I am involved," Novella said quietly, "You are here .. and I am sure there is .. no one else in the neighbourhood who could . . help us discover the names of the whole Gang."

"Whoever discovers it, it should not be you!" Vale said.

Because he spoke so positively, Novella could not help asking:

"Why not . . me?"

He looked at her.

She had the feeling that he was not going to express what was in his thoughts.

Finally he said:

"I can give you an answer to that. It is unnecessary if you do not intend doing what Lord Grimstone has asked."

Novella suddenly felt she was being cowardly. She was not being as brave as the Viscount expected her Father's daughter to be.

"I . . I must make some effort," she said, "to do what has been asked of me . . and if it is . . impossible . . then I will tell . . the Viscount that I have . . failed and perhaps he . . could send somebody else to take my place."

"I think that would be impossible!" Vale said quietly, "and Grimstone will be sharp enough to suspect any stranger who attempts to make his acquaintance."

"Then you . . do see," Novella replied, "that it . . comes back to me."

"I suppose so," he said grudgingly, "but you have to swear to me on everything you hold sacred that you will not allow yourself to be alone with that man. I know his reputation where women are concerned and, as the Viscount said, you must be properly chaperoned."

"I will be .. that, I promise .. you!" Novella assured him.

She was thinking that Miss Graham would be there.

If Lord Grimstone asked her again to visit him, she could insist upon taking Miss Graham with her.

Because she thought it a mistake to go on talking about it, she said in a different tone of voice:

"There is something I must tell you which happened on the journey."

"What was that?" he asked.

"Lord Grimstone obviously got to know I was going to London and sent a spy to follow me."

"I do not believe it," Vale exclaimed. "What did he do?"

Quickly, so as not to upset him Novella told him how the first night the spy had tried to get into her bedroom.

Also she was quite certain he had searched it before.

She went on to relate how on the second night she had changed rooms with Miss Graham.

"That was extremely clever of you," Vale said, "but at the same time I cannot bear to think that this man might have insulted and frightened you."

"He certainly frightened me," Novella said, "but I knew the one thing I had to protect was the letter you had given me."

"I can see that if you were a man you would be immediately enlisted into the Secret Service," Vale said.

"I am sure that is a compliment," Novella smiled, "but it frightened me so much even to think of what you do and what we are doing, I would much rather be fighting on a battlefield without anything secret about it."

Vale laughed.

"You certainly have a point there, and I will try not to let anything like this happen to you again."

He spoke confidently and then he said:

"I suppose if I had really behaved properly I should leave you so that you are no longer under suspicion from that ghastly man."

Novella smiled.

"I think the truth is we have gone so far we cannot now go back. What do you think he will do next?"

"I do not want to think about it, but at the same time we have to be alert and we have to be sensible enough not to take any risks."

Novella could not help thinking that was what she had already done but there was no point in saying so.

She thought that actually however frightening it had been Vale had brought a new impetus into her life which had not been there before.

How could she imagine that he would change everything?

Yet he had, from the moment he had run into the Hall asked for her protection.

Now she could think clearly it had been very exciting to go to London to meet the Viscount Palmerston.

Even to stay a night on the way there had been a change.

The way back had been something new if not so dramatic.

"You are quite right," Vale said and she knew he had been reading her thoughts. "It is good for us all to be roused sometimes into doing what is unusual and to find what we never expected in our lives."

"That is certainly something you are," Novella said, "and I shall never forget when I went down the secret passage and at first I could not see you in the Priests' Hole, I thought you were part of my imagination."

"I thought you were an Angel sent from Heaven," Vale said. "No woman I have ever met before would move so swiftly when I appealed to her for help or conceal me so cleverly."

"We are very lucky to have the secret passage," Novella said, "and I am wondering if we shall want it again."

"I think Dawkins is making absolutely sure that Lord Grimstone's men cannot get into the house," Vale replied, "and nor can Lord Grimstone come unannounced through the front door."

"We can be thankful for that," Novella admitted, "but at the same time I suppose if he does come I shall have to pretend I am pleased to see him."

"If I have my way," Vale said almost harshly, "I will blow the fellow out of the front door and halfway down the drive, before I let him in."

Novella sighed.

"That is what we have got to do, and please you must help me."

He put out his hand.

"You know I will do that."

Shyly she took his hand, and he said:

"How can I thank you for going to London and for taking all these risks on my behalf? A stranger who you have never met before and whom you are now helping."

"You are a soldier," Novella said, "and you know I must as Papa's daughter do anything to help a man who wears the same uniform."

Vale smiled.

"The way Viscount Palmerston spoke," Novella said, "there is no doubt about it, and of course what I should say is that I am very proud to know you."

Vale laughed.

He had taken her hand in his and now he drew her a little nearer.

"You are a very wonderful person," he said, "and one day I will tell you how much I admire you and how grateful I am, but for the moment I have to concentrate on getting well and going back to work."

"You will have to be very careful," Novella said quickly. "If Lord Grimstone can send a man to watch me, I am quite certain whatever you may say that he is still watching you."

"He certainly has been," Vale admitted. "I have, however, a feeling he will begin to be bored by doing so and then perhaps I can think of some way in which you will not even have to meet him."

Novella knew this would interfere with what the Viscount had asked her to do.

She thought however it was a mistake to say anything. Instead she said:

"Now tell me about yourself, you are looking better, much better but Nanny says you have to be careful not to make your arm bleed again."

"Your Nanny has been bullying me as if I were a three-year-old!" Vale complained. "However I have to admit that, thanks to her ministrations and the herbs she makes me drink, I feel far more like my old self again."

"Nanny is wonderful with herbs," Novella said, "and you do look quite different."

She smiled as she spoke.

Then as his eyes met hers he said:

"And you look very lovely! I was so afraid that when London saw you, you would find it boring and return to the country."

Novella flushed at his compliment but said:

"The only person I saw in London was the Viscount and, strangely enough, he did not offer to take me to a Ball!"

"I will take you to one when I am better," Vale promised.

Novella laughed.

"That is a lovely idea, but the only Ballrooms we are likely to find here are the mushroom rings where the fairies have been dancing, and perhaps we can listen to the music of the nightingales."

"One day you shall go to a Ball" Vale promised, "which you would have enjoyed as a débutante, had not the war marooned you here in the middle of nowhere."

"You have been listening to Nanny!" Novella said accusingly. "That is exactly the sort of thing she would say! How could I possibly have a Season in London when Papa is fighting on the Peninsula and Mama is ill because she misses him so much?"

"I know, I know," Vale agreed, "but I promise you, Novella, you shall have your Ball one day, even if you have to wait a little while for it."

"Well, unless you people hurry up and win the

war," Novella retorted, "I shall look very strange with white hair and spectacles, pretending to be a débutante!"

"The war will be over sooner than that," Vale assured her. "In the meantime I am wondering how I can thank you for giving me Sanctuary, which for the moment I dare not leave."

"Of course you cannot leave until you are really well," Novella protested. "And when you do leave you must be very careful how you do so. I do not trust Lord Grimstone not to be snooping about."

"There have certainly been strange shadows in the garden at night," Vale admitted. "But your staff have been very loyal, and on your instructions have refused to allow anybody into the house."

Novella gave a shiver.

"I do not like it," she said. "It makes me shudder to think that outside there are people waiting to kill you. I must show you, as soon as you are well enough to go downstairs, how to open the panel into the secret passage."

"I think I know how to do that," Vale said, "but I would like you to show me, just in case it should become necessary to use it again."

Novella drew in her breath.

"You have not yet told me why Lord Grimstone wishes to kill you."

Vale glanced across the room to see that the door was shut.

Then he said quietly:

"I came back from France in a smuggler's boat. I had no idea when I bribed my way into it where it would take me or for whom the smugglers were working."

"So it was a surprise when you saw Lord Grimstone. Did you know who he was?"

"I recognised him," Vale answered, "and unfortunately, he recognised me."

"So he knew that it meant trouble for him if you informed Viscount Palmerston."

"He knew I would report to London that he was smuggling goods of a high value, and he would consequently be arrested as a traitor."

"I thought," Novella said in a quiet voice, "that it must be . . something like that."

"I am only afraid, now that I am well enough to think clearly," Vale said, "that he may have suspicions about your visit to London."

"I told everybody, including Miss Graham," Novella said, "that it was something Papa had asked me to do."

"That was intelligent of you," Vale smiled, "and I only hope and pray that Grimstone believes it to be the truth."

They talked for a little while longer.

The Nanny came to say that Vale had to go back to bed.

"You've been up long enough, Mr. Vale," she said. "I'm not having you making yerself ill again, just because Miss Novella's come home!"

Vale made a helpless gesture with his right hand.

"You see how I am bullied!" he said. "I can do nothing but what I am told!"

"I should hope not indeed after all the trouble I've taken over you!" Nanny exclaimed. "I began to think I'd never get your temperature down!"

"It is down now," Vale replied, "and tomorrow I shall be able to stay up even longer than I have today."

"We'll see about that!" Nanny said.

It was the sort of answer Nanny would make, Novella thought.

She knew that Vale's eyes were twinkling.

She went from the room so that Nanny would help him off with his robe and get him, as she used to say, 'between the sheets'.

As she went to her bedroom Novella was thinking how charming Vale was, and how thankful she was that Lord Grimstone had been unable to kill him.

"I am sure it would be a terrible loss to England if he succeeded in doing so," she told herself.

Instinctively she went to the window to look out into the garden.

The shadows were growing longer under the trees, and everything seemed quiet and peaceful.

The doves were fluttering towards the dovecot.

The fountain she had loved ever since she was a child was throwing its water towards the sky.

It flickered like a thousand rainbows as it fell back into the stone basin.

It seemed impossible to believe that Wellington's Army was fighting desperately against superior odds.

Here in the peace of England a man like Lord Grimstone was ready to murder anybody who tried to stop him from carrying on his nefarious trade.

'It does not seem real,' Novella thought.

She turned from the window as if the beauty of what she saw outside hurt her.

She dined downstairs with Miss Graham, who talked all through the meal about the change she saw in her Mother.

What Lady Wentmore required she said was to be aroused from her apathy.

"I am certain, my dear," Miss Graham said, "that what your Mother needs is an incentive to make her feel there is something she can do to help your Father."

Novella, who understood what Miss Graham was saying, agreed.

The difficulty was, what could she suggest?

"I must think about it," she replied. "Surely we can find something which will really interest her."

"I will certainly try to do all I can," Miss Graham said. "I love your Mother, I always have, and I cannot bear to think of your Father coming back to find her an invalid."

"I suppose I should have thought of it before," Novella said, "but when she said she just wished to stay in bed, Nanny and I let her, instead of protesting about it."

"You are too young to cope with all this," Miss Graham said, "but I am determined to help your Mother, and I understand you have another invalid on your hands."

Novella looked at her and when Dawkins had left the room she said:

"What have you been told about our guest?"

"I hear he has had an accident and that your Nanny is looking after him," Miss Graham replied. "I also understand he is a young man, and I think it is good for you to have somebody of your own age to talk to."

Novella laughed.

"Oh, Miss Graham," she said, "you are talking just as you did when I was a child! I remember your telling Papa that I should have a girl of my own age with whom to have lessons, so that I should have someone to compete with."

"That was true," Miss Graham agreed, "and you worked very much harder because you wanted to beat Iona, and you also when it suited you enjoyed playing truant with her!"

Novella laughed again.

She was thinking how stupid she had been not to have asked Miss Graham before to come and stay at the Hall.

She had always been so good at arranging other people's lives, even if her own had been a somewhat dull one.

As they finished dinner she said:

"I hope tomorrow, Miss Graham, you will be able to meet our other guest, who, as I expect you have been told, is called Mr. Vale."

"Yes, your Mother told me that," Miss Graham agreed, "and I shall look forward very much to meeting him."

Novella knew from the way she spoke that she was extremely curious about Vale.

However she was far too tactful to ask any uncomfortable questions.

Because they were both tired they went to bed soon after dinner.

As she passed Vale's room, having said goodnight to her Mother, Novella had a sudden longing to talk to him.

She wanted him to tell her what information he had brought back from the Continent with him.

'I do not suppose he will tell me anything as important as that,' she told herself, 'and I shall just have to go on imagining what it might be and making up stories about it.'

In her bedroom she went to the window.

She pulled back the curtains so that she could look up at the stars.

Then she opened the casement a little wider than it was already.

Suddenly she became aware of a movement in the garden below.

It was a very still night with no wind, and yet undoubtedly the leaves of one of the rhododendrons were moving.

Another bush near it did the same thing.

Novella knew then without being told that there was a man in the bushes.

There was no need to question who had sent him, or what he was doing.

He had been ordered to watch the house because Lord Grimstone was still certain that Vale was inside.

In other words he had not given up the chase.

Novella moved away from the window.

She undressed and, as she got into bed, she was shivering.

It was frightening to know they were being watched, and that the men who were doing it were prepared to commit murder.

"Please, God, please .. do not let .. them find him!" she prayed.

She wondered if she should go and warn Vale what was happening outside.

Then she asked herself what was the point.

She was sure this was not the first time that Lord Grimstone's men had been on watch.

They were obviously just waiting for the moment when Vale left the Hall.

Then they would kill him.

"What can we do? How are we to save him?" Novella asked frantically.

Then, almost as if a voice gave her the answer, she knew what should be done.

If Lord Grimstone was arrested first and sent to the Tower of London, then Vale would be safe.

# CHAPTER FIVE

It was nearly a week later when Novella said:

"There is one good thing about it – Lord Grimstone has forgotten about me."

Vale, who was sitting opposite her in the window, smiled.

"Do you really think that is possible?"

"Of course it is possible," she said. "He has never been near me, and I would swear there is no longer anyone lurking in the garden at night."

"You are right about that," Vale said. "But surely you realise Grimstone has just been marking time to see what happens?"

Novella looked at him in surprise, not understanding.

After a moment he explained:

"You can reason it out for yourself that after I escaped from him, thanks to you, he must have expected me to report in London what he was doing and that he would be arrested."

"Yes .. of course .. I realise that .. now," Novella answered.

"He waited, I hope feeling frightened as to what would happen," Vale went on. "Then you went to London."

"I expect he knew about it," Novella said,

"because his men were watching the house, and also no doubt he has agents in the village who tell him everything that is going on."

She shivered but said no more and continued:

"He still has not been arrested, and thinks he has got away with it. Nor, as far as he knows, has anyone been watching the Guinea-Boats moving up to his landing-stage every night."

There was a little pause, before Novella asked:

"And what does he think has happened to you?"

"He is hoping and praying that my wound was far more serious than it was."

"So where does he think you are now?"

"Dead!" Vale replied abruptly. "Or perhaps still too desperately ill to do anything about him. In simple words, the decks are cleared and he can go on with his nefarious trade, and see you again, if that is what he wants to do."

Novella thought for some seconds before she said:

"I can see your reasoning. You think somebody told him I had gone to London on business for Papa, and now he believes it is the truth."

"That is what I think," Vale said, "but of course, he may still be waiting for me, though not, I think here in this house."

Novella could understand that the whole of what Vale had said was a distinct possibility.

In many ways it was a relief.

At the same time, the Guinea-Boats would undoubtedly be unloading, and more and more gold would be reaching France.

"What can we do about it?" Novella asked at length.

"Nothing," Vale replied, "except that I can no longer be cooped up here, and must have some air."

"You are .. not going .. away?" Novella asked.

As she spoke, she knew that if he went away she would feel defenceless and desperately afraid.

There was silence after she had spoken, until she said humbly:

"But of course Viscount Palmerston and the Prime Minister will want to see you in London .. and that is more .. important than anything else."

"I cannot leave you here undefended," Vale said, "but it is difficult for me to know what I can do about your protection."

"But .. I was .. thinking of you," Novella said, "and it .. occurred to me that .. if Lord Grimstone was arrested .. he would no longer .. menace you .. and there would be no more money .. crossing the Channel from .. his house."

The words came rather haltingly, and when she saw the expression on Vale's face she said:

"I have not forgotten what the .. Viscount and the Prime Minister .. wanted me to .. find out .. but I can hardly ask myself to dinner with Lord Grimstone."

"No, of course not!" Vale said curtly. "We will just have to wait a little longer. Then if nothing happens, I will go to London."

Novella felt a wave of relief sweep over her.

She knew that when he left her, she would be very lonely.

There was also something more in what she felt about him which she could not put into words.

It had been very exciting these past few days having someone to talk to.

He told her so many things about the war that she had not understood before.

He also told her about the fascinating countries he had visited.

He had been to Russia.

His descriptions of the Palaces, the Tsar and his family, and many other things he had found there, were captivating.

She realised when she thought it over in bed that he said very little about himself.

He had not yet told her where he lived, if he had a family, and why he was known as 'One-Five'.

Of course she was curious about him.

She would not have been human if she was not.

But she was intelligent enough to realise that there were some things he could not tell her.

She did not want to ask him questions to which he could not give her a reply.

Nanny was very strict that he should still rest.

She also insisted on his having his arm in a sling.

When Novella was doing her usual tasks about the house she counted the minutes until she could go to Vale's room and talk to him again.

Because she feared he might be bored, they also played card-games.

Some of these were those she had enjoyed as a child.

Recently Vale had been certain that there was someone in the garden.

Lord Grimstone was obviously trying to establish if Vale was actually inside the house.

Dawkins had reported that tradesmen had asked questions.

However Mrs. Dawkins was the equal of any inquisitive and, in her mind, impertinent person who ought to mind their own business.

Now Novella was convinced that for the moment the hunt was over.

The difficulty now was what to decide they should do next.

Today Vale had been properly dressed with of course Nanny's permission.

Novella had hurried to his room to show him a book she had found in the library.

It had been written about the smuggling that had taken place in the 17th century.

She knew it would amuse and interest him.

She went into his room to find him sitting in the window.

"I have something to show you," she said, "which I think you will find fascinating."

"What I find fascinating is to see you," he replied, "and I have told Nanny firmly that this is the last day I am going to rest after luncheon. Later in the afternoon when all the gardeners and workmen have gone home, I intend to explore your garden."

"That will be exciting," Novella said. "You are quite sure that you will be safe?"

"I will take every precaution," Vale replied, "and I am wondering if you have a pistol of your Father's that you could lend me."

"Of course I have," Novella answered.

He was wearing her Father's clothes and they were fortunately the same height.

Now that he was no longer wearing the long robe he had a well-tied cravat at his neck.

Novella thought he looked even more handsome than before.

"Do you want me to go and get the pistol now?" she asked. "I know there are three downstairs, two of which are duelling pistols which my Father inherited and, I believe, used to practise with as a young man. The other is a Military pistol which he left behind when he went to Portugal."

"I would like to see them all," Vale said. "But there is no hurry. I cannot go out while the gardeners are there, but I admit I am rather curious about your stables."

"I would like you to see the horses which I drove to London," Novella said, "and also *Heron*, the horse I ride every morning."

"I have been very envious when I hear you going downstairs," Vale said, "and I have longed to be able to join you."

"Perhaps now that we are free of Lord Grimstone's spies, we could ride early in the morning, before anyone is about."

"I will certainly think about it," he promised.

Novella gave him the book about smuggling and he was just opening it when Dawkins appeared.

To Novella's surprise, he came into the room but shut the door behind him before he said:

"Lord Grimstone's here, Miss Novella. Shall I say as you're too busy to see him?"

Novella looked at Vale feeling a streak of fear go through her as she did so.

Just for a moment Vale paused.

She knew without being told that he wanted her to send Lord Grimstone away.

Then he said quietly:

"This is what we have been waiting for. It means we are no longer under surveillance."

Novella gave a deep sigh.

"Very well," she said.

She turned towards Dawkins.

"Show His Lordship into the Drawing-Room, and say I will join him in a few minutes."

Dawkins went from the room.

When he was no longer within ear-shot, Vale said:

"I loathe your having to do this, but, as you promised the Viscount to help, you have to keep your word."

"Yes of course I must," Novella agreed, "but .. you will not go away until .. after I have accepted his .. invitation .. whatever it may be and returned from it?"

"You know I will not do that," Vale answered. "You are very brave Novella, far more brave than any woman I have ever known."

She looked up at him and there was an expression in his eyes that she did not understand.

Then she walked from the room, feeling as she went down the stairs that she was going to the guillotine.

When she opened the door of the Drawing-Room, Lord Grimstone was standing in front of the fireplace.

He was looking even more unpleasant, she thought, than the last time she had seen him.

"How are you, Novella?" he asked as she moved towards him. "You must forgive me if I have been somewhat remiss in not calling on you until now, but I have been extremely busy."

Novella knew that was a lie, but she merely said:

"I think that is what we all are."

"I hope your Mother is better?" Lord Grimstone asked politely.

"I am afraid she will never be really well until Papa returns from the Peninsula," Novella answered. "She worries that he may be .. killed and, as I am sure you are aware, the latest news of Wellington's Army is not very encouraging."

As she spoke she did not look at Lord Grimstone.

She was afraid that he might see the hatred in her eyes for what he was doing.

He was prolonging the war by supplying gold to Napoleon with which he could buy more arms.

"Well, we must not be too down-hearted about things," Lord Grimstone said blithely, "and I feel, my dear Novella, that you need cheering up. That is why I have an invitation for you which is one I hope you will accept."

"What is that?" Novella asked.

"I am giving a dinner-party for a friend of mine, of whom you may have heard. He is Sir Reginald Kershaw, who owns a large Estate in Romney about three or four miles from here."

"I do not .. think I have .. heard of him," Novella said wrinkling her brow.

"He inherited two years ago and is extremely rich, and I think you would enjoy meeting him, together with some of my other friends."

"It is very .. kind of you," Novella said, "but Mama would never allow me to .. accept your invitation .. unless I am properly .. chaperoned."

"Of course you will be," Lord Grimstone

replied. "As it happens, my Aunt, Lady New-combe, will be staying with me, and then going on to Brighton, where she will meet the Prince Regent."

It sounded very respectable and Novella could only say:

"It is very kind of you, My Lord, and I am delighted to accept."

"I am so glad," Lord Grimstone said, "and I know you will not only grace my table, but also delight my friends with your beauty."

There was now a note in his voice and a look in his eyes that made Novella feel frightened.

"Wh.when will your . . dinner-party take place?" she asked.

"I will send a carriage for you tomorrow evening," Lord Grimstone replied, "as I know you will not wish to take your old groom out at night. And you certainly must not drive yourself, as you do so brilliantly, wearing an evening-gown."

He laughed as if at some funny joke, but it told Novella that he knew she had driven to London.

She had to admit that he was right in thinking she would not expect Abbey to take her out at night.

He was getting blind and did not like driving the horses after dark.

"Tomorrow night my carriage will be here at seven o'clock," Lord Grimstone said, "and I shall be counting the hours until then."

He bent forward as he spoke and took her hand in his.

Then, before she could prevent him, he raised it to his mouth.

As she felt his lips hard against the softness of

her skin, she shuddered and tried to take her hand away.

But Lord Grimstone would not let it go.

"You are very lovely, Novella!" he said in a thick voice. "And I not only want to look at you, but also to talk to you when I get the opportunity."

Somehow he made what he said sound sinister.

It was with an almost superhuman effort that Novella prevented herself from saying that was something she did not want, then running away.

Instead she managed to extract her hand without seeming rude.

She forced a smile to her lips before she said:

"Thank you .. very much for the .. invitation. It is very kind of you .. to invite me to .. your house, which I have .. never seen."

"I want to show it to you, and a great many other things as well," Lord Grimstone said.

There was no doubt of the innuendo in his words.

Because Novella could no longer bear his proximity she moved away saying:

"I will go and tell Mama of your kind invitation. I am sure she would have liked to see you, were she well enough."

"I remember your Mother was always a beautiful woman," Lord Grimstone said, "but not as beautiful as you my dear. In fact you are unique in many ways, and that is something we will definitely talk about later."

Novella felt as if he menaced her and took a step backwards.

"Thank you," she said, "but I must not keep .. you when I am .. sure you are .. so busy."

The words seemed to tumble out of her mouth.

Lord Grimstone was aware she was frightened.

There was an ugly expression in his eyes which Novella did not like to interpret to herself.

"Of one thing you may be certain Novella," he said, "I shall never be too busy for you."

At last he started to walk towards the door.

"Give my respects to your Mother," he said, "and tell her I am sure the General will be home soon."

He walked into the hall, but Novella did not follow him. She felt for a moment as if her legs would not support her.

Then she told herself that she had to be sensible about this.

Perhaps at the dinner-party she would learn something which would be of interest to Viscount Palmerston.

She waited until she heard the wheels of Lord Grimstone's carriage moving over the gravel.

When finally there was silence, she knew he had gone.

They had won a victory in that he obviously no longer thought that Vale was hidden in the house.

At the same time she was very afraid of what lay ahead.

"All I have to do," she tried to reassure herself, "is to be sensible and keep my ears and eyes open for something which may help to bring him and his 'gang' to justice."

At the moment it seemed almost an impossible task.

She could not help feeling small and ineffectual.

At the same time she was frightened of Lord Grimstone as a man.

It was not what he said, but something in the tone of his voice and the expression in his eyes.

It made her feel as if he was reaching out towards her and she could not escape him.

It was then she reminded herself that what she was doing would save the lives of British soldiers.

Men who were fighting desperately against a monster who had conquered almost every country in Europe.

If she could save just one man's life by going to dinner with Lord Grimstone, how could she possibly refuse to do so?

Nanny was astonished when Novella told her what she was doing.

"Dine with Lord Grimstone? What ever do you mean by doing such a thing? Your Father never approved of him!"

"I know, Nanny," Novella said, "but there are reasons why I have to go."

"What reasons?" Nanny asked abruptly.

Novella put a hand on Nanny's arm.

"When I went to London," she said, "Viscount Palmerston, the Secretary of State for War, asked me if I would go to Lord Grimstone's house."

"What for?" Nanny inquired.

"Just in case" Novella announced, "there was something I saw or heard there which might prove of use to those who are trying to put an end to the smugglers."

"Smugglers!" Nanny sniffed. "Now what have they got to do with you, I'd like to know? It's disgraceful the way they're behaving! As I have said often enough in the village, it's a crying shame that young boys are creeping across the Channel at night when they should be in their beds!"

"I agree with you, Nanny," Novella said, "and I hear, although of course it may be untrue, that Lord Grimstone is heavily involved."

"If His Lordship's responsible," Nanny said, "then I hope someone drops him in the sea, and he drowns! But that's no reason why you should be mixed up in anything so disgraceful."

"I feel it is something Papa would want me to do," Novella said quietly. "But I think, Nanny, that it would be a great mistake to tell Mama where I am going."

"She wouldn't like it, that's for sure," Nanny agreed, "and I won't have your poor Mother upset – not at this moment when she's feeling so much better having Miss Graham to talk to."

"I was just going to ask you not to tell her either," Novella said, "but of course, Nanny, I never have any secrets from you."

This was sheer flattery, but she knew it was something Nanny enjoyed.

"Oh, very well," Nanny said reluctantly after a moment, "I'll get you ready, and I'll keep where you're going a secret. But you hurry back from that party, and don't stay on one minute after everybody else has gone."

"No, of course not," Novella said. "I would never think of such a thing."

"I don't trust that man, and I never have!" Nanny said. "He's a nasty piece of work from all I hear, so just you be careful not to be left alone with him."

"I certainly would not wish to be that!" Novella agreed.

Grumbling as she did so, Nanny took from the

wardrobe one of Novella's best evening-gowns to press it.

. . . . . . .

The following evening, before she changed, Novella went into her Mother's bedroom to say good-night.

"Nanny says you are tired, Mama," she said, "so I will not come up and disturb you after dinner."

"I have enjoyed today," Lady Wentmore said. "Miss Graham and I were talking about the parties you had when you were small, and what a lot of children there were of your age in the neighbourhood then. I cannot think what has happened to them now!"

"The boys are in the Army," Novella replied, "and most of the girls have married and moved away."

"That is what I hope you will do one day, my darling," Lady Wentmore said. "You must find someone as charming and handsome as your dear Papa, but I am afraid that will be difficult."

"Very difficult, Mama," Novella agreed.

She kissed her Mother goodnight and hurried to her own bedroom.

Nanny was waiting to help her dress.

When Novella was ready she looked, she thought, quite smart in her pretty white muslin gown with silver ribbons crossed under her breasts and falling down behind.

She went to Vale's room.

They had walked in the garden half-an-hour earlier, just as they had done the previous day.

She knew with a sinking of her heart that now

there was nothing to stop him from going to London.

He was standing by the window when she walked in.

He turned round and she thought how handsome he looked in her Father's clothes.

The points of his collar were high above his chin.

"I .. I am .. ready to .. g .. go," she said in a very small voice, "and .. please .. pray for me while I am .. away because I .. I am frightened and .. afraid that all .. this will be for .. n.nothing."

"You cannot do more than try," Vale answered, "but I will certainly be praying, Novella, that you will be safe."

He looked at her again and said, as if he was speaking to himself:

"You are far too lovely to be dining with a swine like Grimstone! I wish you were dining with me."

Novella felt her heart beating faster as she wished that was possible.

She felt shy of her own feelings and said:

"We would .. have to have a .. chaperon with us .. and if it was .. somewhere in this .. neighbourhood .. it would be a question of .. either Nanny .. or Miss Graham."

Vale laughed.

"I was thinking of taking you out to dinner in London," he said, "which of course would be very reprehensible unless we had a party with us."

"I would love to go to a real party in London," Novella said, "but as that is something which is very unlikely to happen, I shall have to .. make do with His Lordship."

"That is a different story altogether," Vale said. "You must just keep listening to what they are saying, and try to see if there is another meaning behind the most ordinary words."

Novella thought this was something he had to do when he was on secret missions.

"I will listen carefully," she promised, "but I wish you were .. coming with me."

Vale smiled.

"Do not forget, His Lordship thinks I am dead, and that he need no longer be afraid of me."

"I will be very .. very careful," Novella answered.

"But above all, of yourself!" Vale emphasised.

To her surprise, he walked across the room and putting his hand under her chin turned her face up to his.

"You are too lovely for this sort of thing," he said roughly, "and far too young!"

Because he was touching her, Novella felt a little thrill run through her.

He was looking at her in a way she did not understand, and she turned towards the door.

"Good-night," she said, "and .. do not .. worry about me."

"That is something I shall certainly be doing," Vale replied.

His voice was hard and, she thought, also angry.

Still very conscious of his touch, she went from the room and down the stairs.

Nanny had found a velvet cape belonging to her Mother and had it ready for her in the hall.

Five minutes later when she was in the Drawing-

Room, Novella heard the sound of the carriage arriving.

She did not wait for Dawkins to tell her it was there, but went out to see that a very smart carriage had been sent for her.

It was drawn by two horses and carried Lord Grimstone's crest on the door.

Dawkins placed the cape over her shoulders.

As she went down the steps the footman got down from the box, opened the carriage door and she stepped in.

As she did so she saw it was very much more luxurious than anything her Father had ever owned.

At the same time she knew that her Mother and she had had to economise because of the war.

Lord Grimstone, however, was making a fortune out of smuggled goods brought over from France.

To think of it made her so angry she felt it surging through her.

Then she told herself that whatever happened, she must bring him to justice.

'I hate him! I hate him!' she thought, remembering it was what she had said the first time she met him.

It seemed to her that the carriage wheels as they drew her along the road towards Lord Grimstone's house were repeating over and over again:

"I hate him! I hate him! I hate him!"

# CHAPTER SIX

Lord Grimstone's house was far larger than Novella had expected.

But as she looked around her she thought it was not furnished in particularly good taste.

However, as she followed the Butler across a large hall, she was aware that there were an inordinate number of servants on duty.

The Drawing-Room, to her surprise was upstairs on the First Floor.

As she entered she saw it was a very large room with windows overlooking the sea.

There were several people there already.

As she was announced Lord Grimstone came towards her.

She thought that even in his evening-clothes, in which she had always admired her Father, he looked unpleasant.

When he pressed her hand and held it for too long, she knew that she was frightened as well as feeling hatred for him.

He introduced her to his other guests.

First there was his Aunt, Lady Newcombe, who was obviously very old.

Yet to Novella's surprise she was heavily made

up with darkened eye-lashes, pink cheeks and red lips.

"So this, Herbert, is the pretty little chicken you have been telling me about!" she said in a cackling voice.

One of the other guests laughed.

It proved to be Sir Reginald Kershaw, who was not in the least the sort of man Novella had expected him to be.

He looked rather like an underhead clerk.

She was to learn later he had in fact worked in one of the Ministries in London before he retired.

There were four other men present, all of whom were middle-aged and lived in the neighbourhood.

One had a house in Dover, another like Sir Reginald in Romney.

The other two identified themselves as being not far down the coast.

They were all drinking champagne.

As it was something Novella had had only as a treat at Christmas time, she sipped it slowly.

They were all laughing at jokes she did not understand.

They went on drinking for a long time and she thought they seemed unlikely to say anything that would be of interest to Viscount Palmerston.

When they went into dinner, Lady Newcombe sat at the end of the table.

Novella found herself on Lord Grimstone's right.

He kept paying her fulsome compliments in a thick voice.

Long before dinner was finished she became more and more frightened and hoped she would be able to get away as quickly as possible.

There were however a large number of courses.

The food was excellent but Novella realised as course succeeded course that nearly every dish was French.

They were drinking French champagne, then there was French wine and finally French brandy.

There was a pâté which could only have come from France.

In another course there were truffles, which she recognised even though she had never eaten them before.

She was sure they too had crossed the Channel.

It seemed to her that the men ate enormously.

She found it impossible to eat more than just a little of each of the dishes she was offered.

Lord Grimstone, who was watching her, said:

"I see you are very thin, Novella. Is that because you are slimming, like so many other stupid women? Or do you not have the sort of food at home that you are enjoying here?"

"I am certainly not slimming!" Novella answered, "and of course, My Lord, the food is delicious. But now that my Father is away, I am not used to very large meals."

"That is what I will give you when you come here to me," Lord Grimstone said.

He spoke as if it would be a frequent occurrence, and it was with difficulty that Novella did not shudder.

She heard Sir Reginald, who was at the other side of Lord Grimstone, say:

"I find your food excellent, and I am also very grateful for what I can enjoy in my own house."

Novella noticed that he dropped his voice when he said the last words.

He also gave Lord Grimstone a knowing look.

She was at the moment sure that he was part of the smuggling ring she was trying to identify.

The four servants who were waiting on them filled up his glass every time a man took even a sip of wine.

By the end of dinner the gentlemen's voices had thickened.

They also seemed to speak more loudly and continuously laughed at their own jokes.

At the other end of the table Lady Newcombe was laughing too.

Novella saw her slap the hand of the man on her right.

It was as if she was rebuking him for something he had said which was outrageous.

'I am hating this party,' Novella thought, 'and the sooner I can go home, the better.'

Then she told herself that she must be more attentive to what they were saying.

If Sir Reginald was in league with Lord Grimstone, she thought the other men present probably were also.

As dinner drew to a close one of them raised his glass to say:

"I think we should all drink to our host and be very grateful to him for all the kindnesses he has shown us."

"Hear! Hear!" the other men responded.

Lord Grimstone sat back in his chair with a smile of satisfaction on his face.

"You can thank me again when you get home tonight," he said.

Novella thought there was a glint of excitement in the eyes of the men listening.

Then they raised their glasses once again and drank until they were empty.

Later they were drinking brandy when, somewhat reluctantly, Lady Newcombe said:

"I think we ladies should move to the Drawing-Room."

"We will not be long," Lord Grimstone replied.

Novella, who had been longing to move for sometime, sprang quickly to her feet.

As she would have passed Lord Grimstone, he put out a hand to touch hers.

"I will not leave you longer than I can help, my beautiful one," he said, "for I have a lot to say to you."

Novella wanted to reply that she would like to go home, but thought it a mistake to say so at that moment.

Instead she followed Lady Newcombe out of the Dining-Room, through the hall and up the stairs.

When they reached the Drawing-Room, two large crystal chandeliers had been lit.

Novella had to admit that it looked attractive, but not at all as pretty as her Mother's Drawing-Room.

She walked across the room to the window.

The curtains had not been drawn, and now the stars were coming out over the sea.

There was a moon throwing its light on the waves.

It was exquisitely lovely.

It was difficult to realise that the men downstairs were making use of that sea for making money, and were traitors to their own country.

Because she did not want to think of that at the moment, Novella turned away.

She found to her surprise that she was alone in the Drawing-Room.

She thought perhaps Lady Newcombe had gone to tidy herself.

Yet the minutes ticked by and she did not re-appear.

Novella wondered if she had retired to bed without saying goodnight.

In which case, she thought uncomfortably, she had no chaperon.

"As soon as the Gentlemen come from the Dining-Room, I will say I must leave," she told herself.

She went back to the window to look again at the stars and the sea.

It seemed a long time, but it must have been only about a quarter-of-an-hour before she heard the voices of the men.

They were at last coming out of the Dining-Room.

She stood waiting, finding it impossible to sit down.

After a few minutes she moved about looking at the pictures, none of which were by any well-known artist.

Then she inspected a large cabinet, in which there was displayed an indifferent collection of china.

Her Mother had taught her how to recognise antiques when she saw them.

She had a feeling that everything in the room had been bought recently by Lord Grimstone.

Nothing had been passed down through the centuries as everything in her own home had been.

At last, when she was beginning to think that she had been forgotten, the door opened.

Lord Grimstone came in.

She turned from the china cabinet to say:

"I think, My Lord, that Her Ladyship has retired to bed, and therefore I must go home."

"There is no hurry," Lord Grimstone said in a thick voice and walked towards her. "I have seen my other guests off so that I could have the opportunity of talking alone to a very beautiful young lady."

Novella drew in her breath.

"That is something of which my Mother would disapprove," she said quickly, "so please, My Lord, may I leave now?"

"As I have already said, there is no hurry," he replied. "I have been counting the hours until this moment, when I could tell you how lovely you are."

Novella shivered.

The way he was looking at her frightened her more than ever.

"Please .. please," she pleaded, "I must .. go. My Mother is .. expecting me."

"So you are frightened of me!" Lord Grimstone said.

The way he spoke told Novella it was something that pleased him.

Then, with unexpected suddenness, he put out his arms and pulled her close to him.

"You excite me!" he said. "I find your beauty and your innocence irresistible!"

Novella realised with horror that he was about

to kiss her. She struggled and tried with all her strength to push him away.

"So you want to fight me, do you?" he asked with a chuckle. "Well, that is something I will enjoy! But you may be quite sure, my fluttering little Dove, that I shall be the victor!"

"Leave .. me .. alone! You .. are .. not to .. touch me!" Novella cried.

There was a smile on his thick lips as he drew closer and still closer.

His arms were like bands of steel and she was completely helpless in his grasp.

He held her so close against his chest that she could hardly breathe.

Then as his lips sought hers, she twisted her head from side to side.

Finally, as his mouth was against her cheek, she gave a scream of terror.

Even as she did so, the door opened and a man's voice said:

"*Bonsoir, cher ami*! I breeng *les lettres* of great import. *Voila*!"

Entering the room behind a servant who had opened the door there came a man.

He was wearing a long black cape and a soft black hat was pulled low over his forehead.

In his outstretched hand he held two letters.

He had a curled moustache which seemed in keeping with his foreign appearance.

Lord Grimstone was so taken by surprise that his grip on Novella slackened. Swiftly she moved away from him.

By this time the Frenchman was half-way across the room and the servant had shut the door behind him.

134

"What is this? Who are you?" Lord Grimstone began to demand.

"*Voici vos lettres, Monsieur,*" the Frenchman said, thrusting them into his hand, "and I have too *un message pour vous.*"

As he spoke he bent his head towards Lord Grimstone, who was staring at him.

Swiftly, the Frenchman struck him a blow on the chin which lifted him into the air.

Then he crashed backwards on to the ground.

Because it was such a surprise, Novella gave a little cry of horror.

Then in a low voice the Frenchman said:

"It is all right, my darling, but be very quiet. We do not want to attract attention."

It was Vale! Vale!

Novella had not of course recognised him as he came into the room looking so strange.

She watched as Vale took from his pocket a silk handkerchief with which he gagged his unconscious victim.

Then swiftly he tied his wrists and ankles with short ropes which he produced from inside his cloak.

He moved the sofa slightly, which stood in front of one of the windows.

Then he dragged the unconscious man behind it and pushed it back into place.

Smiling he came towards Novella.

"You .. are .. here!  You .. are .. here!" she whispered incoherently. "I was .. so frightened .. and then .. you .. came!"

"You should have trusted me," Vale said, "and now we have to get out of this mess!"

He looked down at her.

Her eyes were very wide, but no longer dark with fear as they had been when he had first come into the room.

Bending his head, he gently touched her lips with his.

She felt a thrill like a streak of lightning sweep through her.

But before she could comprehend that Vale had kissed her, he said:

"Now listen, my precious, we have to get out of this house and if the servants downstairs know who I am, they will kill me! So just agree with everything I say, and look happy as if you are enjoying yourself."

It was an order.

Novella tried to concentrate on what he was saying and forgot the rapturous feeling that had made her heart turn a somersault.

He pulled his soft black hat lower and walked towards the door.

"Now, smile," he commanded, "and wave good-bye to your host."

He opened the door as he spoke, saying in a loud voice with a French accent:

"*Bonne nuit, mon ami*! Enjoy zee *lettres* an' I weel talk wiz *vous* about them tomorrow."

Novella raised her hand and said:

"Goodnight, My Lord, and thank you so much!"

She thought her voice sounded quite natural although, because she was so nervous, she was trembling.

Vale shut the door behind them and they walked unhurriedly down the stairs.

When they reached the bottom, Novella saw there were four men in the hall.

They were the Butler and three footmen, who all looked too strong and coarse to be ordinary servants.

Vale spoke to the Butler.

"*Monsieur* your Master," he said, "ask me take *Mademoiselle* wiz me an' see 'er 'ome. He eez verry beezy wiz letters an' do not disturb *Monsieur* unteel 'e call – you understand?"

"I understand, Sir," the Butler replied.

"I take *Mademoiselle*," Vale said, smiling beneath his moustache, "een my boat. A carriage eez waiting up ze coast."

He pointed to the West.

"Then if you will come with me, Sir," the Butler said, "I will show you the way."

He walked ahead and Vale said:

"Ah, *oui*, I recall when *j'arrive*."

They went down a long passage, then through a heavy door to where there were a number of steps going down.

Novella realised they ended at sea-level.

She had been aware when she arrived that Lord Grimstone's house had been built on a cliff above the sea.

She thought that it must originally have been a Watchtower or a fortification to which the rest of the building had been added later.

As they started to walk down the steps, Vale said to the Butler who was still accompanying them:

"*Maintenant*, I find ze way. *Merci beaucoup* for *votre attention*."

He pressed some money into the man's hand,

137

who took it greedily. As they continued down the steps he did not follow them.

Now Vale held Novella's hand and she felt his fingers close over hers.

She was trembling, knowing that the men in the hall would have shot Vale if they realised who he was.

Aware that they were still in danger, Vale quickened his pace.

There was just enough light on the steps for them to see.

It came from a lantern at the top and the moonlight at the bottom.

Novella saw that the lowest steps ended in a huge sea-cavern.

There was a boat with twelve oarsmen at what was a perfect underground Quay.

It might have been specially built for smugglers.

As they appeared, one of the men got out of the boat.

Vale said to him in a low voice:

"Is everything all right, Tom?"

"They be under lock and key, Sir," the man replied, "an' we've exchanged what we found 'ere with what we brought."

"Good!" Vale said.

He picked Novella up in his arms and lowered her gently into the boat.

Then he followed her, sitting beside her.

The man they had been talking to sprang aboard and picked up his oar.

They did not wait for Vale to give the order, but started to manoeuvre out of the cavern.

As they did so, Novella saw there was a pile of packing-cases on a ledge.

She realised, too, that the bow of the boat was heavy with cases.

She did not understand, she just noticed it, that they were unopened, as the boat came out of the cavern.

The twelve men started to row very swiftly, first out to sea, then turning Southwards.

Vale did not speak, but he was still holding Novella's hand.

She could only think of how, by a miracle, he had saved her from Lord Grimstone's clutches.

At the same time it seemed incredible that he was actually there.

He had disguised himself as a Frenchman, and there were a hundred questions she wanted to ask him.

At the moment, however, she felt as if the whole thing was a dream.

Nothing was real except the pressure of his fingers.

They must have been rowing for about half-an-hour before they drew into the shore.

There was a small bay, apparently unoccupied.

The oarsmen beached the boat and Tom, who had spoken to them before, got out first.

He was wearing long fishing-boots, and he walked through the water to where Novella was sitting.

"Tom will carry you ashore," Vale said quietly.

Novella stood up and was put down softly on the sand.

A minute later Vale joined her.

He had a small bag in his hand which she guessed contained money.

He handed it to Tom saying:

"Thank you, Tom, for the brilliant way in which you have tonight struck a blow against a lot of dirty traitors. I hope they will swing for what they have been doing for far too long."

"Oi' hopes so too, Sir," Tom said, "an' oi' thank you on behalf o' us all."

Vale shook his hand, then to Novella's surprise, picked her up in his arms.

He carried her across the sand and up a small twisting path. It led to the top of the cliff, which was not high.

When they reached it Novella saw there was a carriage a little way from them drawn by four horses.

As they appeared a footman jumped down from the box and opened the carriage-door.

Vale put Novella on the back seat, then climbed in beside her.

The door was shut and the horses moved off.

Then as he pulled off the felt hat he wore, followed by the false moustache, Novella gave a cry.

"You .. saved .. me! Oh .. Vale! How could .. you have .. done it?"

The words seemed to fall from her lips.

Then, as if it was all too much for her, she found the tears were running down her cheeks.

Vale put his arms around her.

"It is all right, my Darling," he said. "It is all over. We have won and before that swine regains consciousness, the soldiers will have moved in and it will be over for the rest of them."

"I .. I do not .. understand," Novella sobbed, "but you .. are .. here! H.How could you .. have been so .. clever to .. c.come just when I .. I needed .. y.you?"

140

Her voice broke again on the words, but Vale did not answer.

Instead he put his fingers under her chin and turned her face up to his.

Then he was kissing her.

Not gently as he had done before, but fiercely and possessively as if he were afraid he might lose her.

Soon Novella was no longer crying.

Instead she was pulsating with a rapture she had never known at the wonder of Vale's kisses.

He kissed not only her lips, but her eyes, her little straight nose, her cheeks, then once again he took possession of her mouth.

"I love you!" he said, "God, how I love you, and I thought it was something I would never be able to tell you."

"W.Why . . ?" Novella asked.

"I had nothing to offer you, my Darling, but a man who if he stepped out of the sanctuary into which you had taken him would have died ignominiously."

"I cannot . . bear to think . . of it," Novella murmured. "But . . now you are all . . right? It does not hurt your arm to . . come out tonight?"

Vale did not answer, and after a moment she went on:

"Those men . . might have . . shot at . . you again!"

"I had to take the risk," Vale said quietly. "Now we are safe and Grimstone's men will not be looking for me any more."

"Are you sure . . really . . sure?" Novella asked.

Now she was frightened again and she put her hand on Vale's chest, as if she would protect him.

"It is all right, my Precious," he said.

"But Lord Grimstone's men might have .. recognised you!"

"*You* might have done that," he said gently, "and by showing surprise, might have given the game away."

"But .. you deceived me completely," Novella said. "How could I imagine for one moment that you would appear in Lord Grimstone's house when you knew he was trying to .. k.kill you?"

She gave a sob as she added, "Then you acted so brilliantly that .. he did not know .. who you .. were."

Vale laughed.

"I am rather proud of myself," he said.

"But .. you came .. alone, and any of .. those men might have .. suspected it was .. you," Novella murmured.

"I trusted in my Guardian Angel, who of course, is you, to save me," Vale said, "and you have not only done that, my Darling, but Viscount Palmerston and the Prime Minister will be very pleased with us."

"I am sure .. the men at the .. dinner party were .. all part of Lord Grimstone's gang," Novella said, "but I could .. not .. prove it."

"There is no need for you to do so," Vale said, "I am certain that each one of them will take home with him a case of either champagne or brandy! When the soldiers apprehend them, they will be discovered to have smuggled goods in their possession."

"Oh .. that is clever .. so clever of .. you!" Novella exclaimed.

"That is what I want you to think," Vale said.

"But the thing I am proudest of is that I got you away from that devil before he could kiss you."

"I . . I was . . fighting him . . but he was s.so . . strong," Novella whispered.

"Now tell me that I am the only man who has ever kissed you," Vale said.

"I . . I had . . no idea . . until you . . kissed me . . that a kiss . . could be so . . wonderful," Novella said softly.

Then Vale was kissing her again.

Kissing her until she felt as if the moon and the stars had invaded the carriage and were moving within her breast.

All her dreams had come true.

# CHAPTER SEVEN

A long time later, Novella stirred in Vale's arms and asked:

"Surely we .. should be .. home by .. now?"

"You are not going home," he answered.

She gave a little gasp of surprise.

"Mama will be .. anxious if I do not .. return."

"I have explained to your Mother that I am taking you to my home," Vale said.

"Y.you .. explained to .. Mama? Then .. you have told her that .. I was with .. Lord Grimstone!"

"I told her that you had gone to dine with him because you believed you would be helping England in the war. She said immediately that she was sure it was what your Father would want you to do."

Novella gave a little sigh of relief.

"I feel .. however," she said nervously, "that .. she will be .. worried when I .. do not come .. home."

"I cannot take the risk of some of Grimstone's men avoiding arrest," Vale explained, "and coming in search of you and me."

"I .. I had forgotten they .. might do that," Novella said.

Now she was frightened and she clung to the lapel of his coat as she said:

"You are safe .. you promise me .. you will be safe .. and they will not .. attack you .. again."

"I think that is very unlikely," Vale said, "and certainly not where I am taking you."

"Where .. are you taking .. me?" Novella asked. "I am so .. bewildered by .. everything that has .. happened – you .. disguised as .. a Frenchman .. the boat .. and now this .. smart carriage .. that I have not been .. able to .. think."

"All I want you to think about," Vale said, "is that I love you."

He pressed his lips against her forehead as he spoke.

It was not a passionate kiss, but Novella felt as if a little flame seeped through her.

"I suppose," Vale said a moment later, "that I had better tell you the whole story from the beginning. Then we can forget it, and think only of ourselves."

"Yes .. tell me .. please .. tell me," Novella said. "I am .. completely .. bewildered as I have been ever since .. you ran into .. the hall and asked me to .. save your .. life."

Vale laughed.

"It must have seemed somewhat unusual, I admit that."

"I was so .. terrified that those .. men would .. wound you .. again," Novella said.

Because she remembered the fear that had been with her all the evening, she hid her face against his shoulder.

He held her tightly against him and said:

"Now I will start our Fairy Story, which has a very happy ending."

"That is .. what I .. want to .. hear," Novella whispered.

"When you came back from London," Vale began, "and told me what the Prime Minister and Viscount Palmerston had asked of you, I knew that you would be in danger. You might have been hurt. You would certainly be the object of Lord Grimstone's attentions, and even be disposed of if his suspicions were aroused."

His arms tightened as he said:

"When I saw you in that man's arms, he was lucky that I did not kill him there and then!"

There was a fierceness in Vale's voice which Novella found very exciting.

Then he went on:

"Because it was what I anticipated I wrote to Viscount Palmerston and told him what I wanted."

"You .. wrote to him?" Novella questioned. "How did you do .. that?"

"I thought perhaps that would surprise you," Vale said, "but actually I wrote an ordinary letter and sent it by post."

"I .. I never .. thought of you doing .. that when you sent .. me to London with your .. note to him .. in code."

"That was something rather different," Vale said, "since it was of the utmost importance that it should reach the War Office as quickly as possible."

He gave a sigh.

"I had been delayed in finding a smuggler's boat to bring me to England, and further delayed by

146

being captured by Grimstone's men and then being wounded in escaping from them."

"I cannot .. bear to .. think they .. might have .. killed you!" Novella said in a low voice.

"I am very much alive, my Precious," Vale said in a tone of satisfaction.

He kissed her forehead again before he continued:

"In my letter to Viscount Palmerston I asked for a man proficient in reading Morse Code by candlelight to be in your wood every night after dark."

Novella was astonished.

"Why should you want .. that?" she asked.

"Because I knew that once Lord Grimstone had decided I was either dead or else too ill to denounce him as a smuggler, he would ask you to dinner."

"I can .. see how .. you worked it all .. out," Novella said, "but .. why a man who .. knew Morse Code?"

"To tell him the moment you knew the actual night on which you were dining with that devil, so that my plan to rescue you could be put into operation."

"You .. you mean the .. boat in which .. you arrived .. so unexpectedly?" Novella said hesitatingly.

"Exactly!" Vale agreed.

"But .. how could you .. do anything .. so risky that .. if they had .. guessed who you were .. you would have died?"

There was a note of horror in her voice which Vale found very touching.

"Nothing was too risky where it concerned

you," he said quietly, "and I knew also it would give the Viscount the information he required."

"You .. guessed that the .. men dining with .. him would be .. his gang?" Novella asked.

"I thought it very likely," Vale replied, "if they dined with Lord Grimstone, they would take some of the spoils home with them while the rest would be left in the cavern to be collected by those who were taking it to London to be sold."

"How could .. you be .. so clever!" Novella exclaimed.

"Because it concerned you," Vale replied, "it was the most important mission I have ever undertaken, and one I had to win!"

Novella gave a little murmur and pressed her cheek against his shoulder.

"I was right," he said, "because when the men took me into the cavern tonight we found a great pile of goods which had just been delivered from France. When I had gone into the house to rescue you, the men in my boat exchanged the cases for the ones we had brought with us."

"And what did they contain?" Novella enquired.

"Stones!" Vale replied with a smile.

She laughed and he said:

"When the packages were being exchanged, Tom and the other men in my boat seized Grimstone's servants. They tied them up so that they could not escape and hid them in another cavern where they will be found by the soldiers."

"How .. can you have .. thought of .. every detail?" Novella asked in an awe-stricken voice.

"I had plenty of time when you were not with me," Vale answered, "and because it was so demanding, it is something I hope never to have to do again."

"And now .. you are safe .. completely and .. absolutely safe."

"Only if you will look after me and take care of me, and of course hide me when I have to be hidden, although, as I told you before, I have no secret passages in my house."

Novella looked up at him.

"Is that where we are going, to your house?"

"It is halfway between Wentmore Hall and London," Vale said, "and although it is very different from your house, I am hoping you will admire it."

"Of course I shall!" Novella said. "But I am still .. worrying a .. little about .. Mama."

"I promise you, I made what I had to do seem quite simple, and I told her that while I was taking you to my home, you would be chaperoned by my grandmother, who has been staying there to look after everything while I was abroad."

He paused for a moment. Then he said:

"I have also suggested to your Mother something of which I think you will approve."

"What is .. that?" Novella enquired.

"When I told her where I was going, and how important it was, Nanny was with her, and also Miss Graham," Vale answered. "I told them that Lord Grimstone, having been shot as a traitor, or imprisoned for life in the Tower of London, his house would be empty."

Novella wondered why this was of any particular importance.

"It is a large house," Vale went on, "and I understand we should be grateful for the fact that he has no heir. It can therefore be confiscated by the Crown."

Novella was puzzled, but she did not speak and he continued.

"I therefore intend to suggest to Viscount Palmerston that it is turned into a Hospital for the men who have been wounded fighting with Wellington's Army which will soon be in France."

"A Hospital!" Novella exclaimed.

"It is something which I am afraid a great number of men will need," Vale went on, "and I suggested to your Mother that she should run it and supervise everything, helped of course by Miss Graham and Nanny!"

Novella gave a little cry.

"I do not .. believe it! But, it is a .. wonderful idea! I am certain it is something Mama would .. want to do."

"She agreed at once," Vale said, "and I think when your Father returns, which I hope will be next year at the very latest, he will find your Mother on her feet again and looking exactly as he remembered her when he went away."

Novella put her arms around Vale's neck.

"How can .. you be so .. clever and so .. brilliant as to think of something which will not only interest Mama, but also make her .. well again! Oh, thank you, thank you. You are .. wonderful!"

Vale kissed her.

As she clung to him she felt the horses slowing down.

"We are home!" Vale said quietly, "and now, Darling, I promise you we are both completely and absolutely safe. I will tell you the rest of my story once we are inside."

The carriage came to a standstill and through the window Novella saw a flight of stone steps down which had been run a red carpet.

Footmen wearing a smart livery came down the steps to open the carriage door.

Vale stepped out first, then helped Novella to alight.

Holding her hand, they walked together up the steps flanked on each side by a Heraldic device in stone.

Novella had only had a quick glance at the house.

Yet she could see it was very large and the moonlight glittered on what seemed to her to be a hundred windows.

Then she was inside the magnificent hall with a very fine staircase with banisters of crystal and gold.

An elderly Butler with white hair was bowing to Vale.

"Welcome home, M'Lord!" he said.

"It has been a long time, Watson," Vale answered, "but it is delightful to be back."

"There's champagne and sandwiches in the Drawing-Room, M'Lord," Watson informed him. "Her Grace has retired to bed knowing you'd understand."

"Yes, of course," Vale replied. "I had no idea of exactly when we would be arriving, and it would have been too much for Her Grace to wait up for us."

As he was speaking the Butler was walking

ahead of them towards the door of a room on the other side of the hall.

Feeling bemused by what was happening, Novella was holding tightly onto Vale's hand.

He led her into an enormous room, one of the most attractive she had ever seen.

Huge chandeliers glittered with lighted candles.

She also recognised that the fireplace and the gilt furniture were perfect examples of the work of the Adam brothers.

Her Mother had always said that next to their Elizabethan house, there was nothing she admired more than the Palladian architecture of the previous century.

Vale walked to a table in the corner of the room.

On it Novella saw there was a bottle of champagne in a gold ice-bucket.

He poured out two glasses.

As he handed one to Novella, the Butler having seen that they had everything they required, left the room.

"Now my Precious," Vale said, "we can drink to our happiness."

"Is this *your* house?" Novella asked, "and the Butler . . called you . . 'My Lord'."

"Now at last I can tell you the truth," Vale replied. "I am the Earl of Harchester, and my maternal grandmother, who is chaperoning you, is the Dowager Duchess of Longleat."

Novella gave a little gasp.

"Then . . you are . . very grand!" she exclaimed. "And this house . . seems enormous!"

"I want you to love it as much as I do," Vale said, "and now, my Darling, at last, and it seems as if I have waited a long, long time, I can ask you to marry me."

Novella stared at him.

Gently he took the glass from her hand and put it down on the table.

Then he pulled her very close to him.

"I cannot tell you," he said, "how frustrating it has been to see you day after day, and not tell you how much I love you and how desperately I wanted to kiss you."

He did not wait for her reply, but kissed her as he had before.

It was not gently, but demandingly, and possessively, until his kiss became passionate.

It was as if he swept Novella once again into the sky.

Only when Vale released her did she manage to say a little incoherently:

"D.did you..really..ask me to..m.marry you?"

"I have every intention of marrying you," he said, "because quite simply, my Lovely One, I cannot live without you. I want you to protect me, take care of me and make this house a Fairytale Palace of happiness."

He smiled before he added turning her face up to his:

"I have told you my story and it must end with 'they lived happily ever after'."

Novella's face was radiant.

Then suddenly, to his surprise, she hid her face against his neck saying:

"I..I love you..you know I I.love you..but I do not..think I can..m.marry you."

She felt him stiffen.

"Why not? What do you mean?" he asked. "How could you kiss me like that and yet say you do not want to marry me?"

"I love you .. with all my .. heart and with .. all my soul," Novella said pathetically, "but .. if you .. went away .. again on one of those .. dangerous journeys on which you might be .. k.killed at any moment .. with other men like .. Lord Grimstone .. wanting to destroy you .. I think .. I would .. d.die!"

She gave a little sob.

"I would end up like .. Mama .. getting weaker and weaker because Papa is fighting with Wellington's Army."

The way she spoke made Vale acutely aware of the agony in her voice.

"My Darling, my Sweet," he said, "do you really think I would make you suffer in such a way?"

His arms tightened as he said:

"There is something else I am going to tell you, but perhaps I should have told you it first, before I asked you to be my wife."

"What .. is it?" Novella asked.

He could feel her trembling in his arms and he knew it was because her love for him was so intense that she would always be afraid when he was out of her sight.

"What I have to tell you," he said quietly, "is that in the letter I received from Viscount Palmerston confirming that everything I had asked for would be done, he added something else."

"Wh.what was that?" Novella questioned.

"He said that now that I was a marked man, there would be no more secret missions for me in the future. But he said my knowledge and experience would be of tremendous value in the War Office. He has therefore offered me the position as Minister of State for War."

As he finished speaking he knew that Novella was suddenly very still.

Then as she raised her head to look up at him there were tears in her eyes.

He thought he had never seen a woman look more beautiful or more in love.

"D.do you .. m.mean .. do you r.really mean," she stammered, "that .. you will .. be .. working in .. L.London?"

"I will be in London – with you!" Vale said simply. "So my Darling, you now have no excuse not to be my wife."

"Oh, Vale, if you were .. in London I would not be .. frightened for .. you, but you must swear that you will be very .. very .. careful, because until the war .. has ended .. I will always .. be afraid that .. something might .. happen to .. you."

"Nothing will happen," Vale said quietly, "except that I shall be married to the sweetest, most adorable woman in the whole world!"

He pulled her a little closer to him.

Then he said:

"Now, answer my question – how soon will you marry me?"

"Now! At once!" Novella cried. "At this very moment! Oh, Vale .. Vale, I love .. you! And I .. know we .. will be very .. happy."

"Wildly, blissfully, perfectly happy!" Vale said. "And we will be married, my Darling, by my private Chaplain, as soon as I can get a Special Licence."

He saw a little flicker of hesitation in Novella's eyes and added:

"I told your Mother before I left that I would send a carriage for her and of course Miss Graham and Nanny."

"And she . . agreed?" Novella asked.

"Before I left she was already deciding which gown she would wear," Vale said with laughter in his voice.

"I . . do not . . believe it!" Novella said. "You are not just . . very clever . . you are positively a Magician! And for me you are the Archangel Michael, who . . came down from . . Heaven to save . . me when I . . thought I was . . completely and absolutely . . lost."

Vale gave a little laugh.

Then his lips were on hers.

As he held Novella tightly against him, he knew the last obstacle had fallen.

He had won what had been a long and complicated campaign.

He had known even as he planned everything so carefully that one false move, one slip, could spell disaster!

By the mercy of God, however, he had succeeded.

Now he had been lucky enough to find the one woman in the world that he had ever wanted to be his wife.

"I love you, Novella!" he said. "I love you so much that there are no words to express what I feel for you. It may take perhaps a hundred years before I can tell you adequately how much I love you."

"And I . . love . . you," Novella whispered. "You

156

are so . . marvellous . . so wonderful and . . clever. At the same time so kind and . . understanding. Oh, Vale . . Vale . . how lucky . . we are!"

"We have been blessed," Vale said quietly. "Right has triumphed over wrong, and good over evil. That, my Precious Adorable One, is what we must aim for all our lives here in our home and for our country."

He spoke solemnly, which made Novella look at him wide-eyed.

Then she said:

"I am sure . . no other man would . . say that, and it is . . one of the . . reasons why I . . love you so . . much. Oh . . Vale . . I shall pray and . . pray that I will . . never lose . . you."

"And I know that your prayers will be answered," Vale said.

Then he was kissing her again.

Then they were both aware of a light that surrounded them which was not of this world.

It was a light that came not only from Heaven, but also from their hearts and minds.

It had carried them through every danger until they were safely together.

It was love, the love that had protected them.

The love which is not only human, but Divine.

It would be theirs throughout their lives and in other lives to come.

It was the love which came from God and which goes on to Eternity.

# Other Books by Barbara Cartland

**Other Novels, over 500, the most recently published being:**

The Duke is Trapped
Just a Wonderful Dream
Love and a Cheetah
Drena and the Duke
A Dog, A Horse and A Heart
Never Lose Love
Spirit of Love
The Eyes of Love
The Duke's Dilemma
Saved by a Saint

Beyond the Stars
The Innocent Imposter
The Incomparable
The Dare-Devil Duke
The Royal Rebuke
The Love Light of Apollo
Love Light of the Gods
Love, Lies and Marriage
In Love in Lucca
The Perfection of Love

The Dream and the Glory (In aid of the St. John Ambulance Brigade)

**Autobiographical and Biographical:**

The Isthmus Years 1919–1939
The Years of Opportunity 1939–1945
I Search for Rainbows 1945–1976
We Danced All Night 1919–1929
Ronald Cartland (With a foreword by Sir Winston Churchill)
Polly – My Wonderful Mother
I Seek the Miraculous

**Historical:**

Bewitching Women
The Outrageous Queen (The Story of Queen Christina of Sweden)
The Scandalous Life of King Carol
The Private Life of Charles II
The Private Life of Elizabeth, Empress of Austria
Josephine, Empress of France
Diane de Poitiers
Metternich – The Passionate Diplomat
A Year of Royal Days
Royal Jewels
Royal Eccentrics
Royal Lovers

## Sociology:

| | |
|---|---|
| You in the Home | Etiquette |
| The Fascinating Forties | The Many Facets of Love |
| Marriage for Moderns | Sex and the Teenager |
| Be Vivid, Be Vital | The Book of Charm |
| Love, Life and Sex | Living Together |
| Vitamins for Vitality | The Youth Secret |
| Husbands and Wives | The Magic of Honey |
| Men are Wonderful | The Book of Beauty and Health |

Keep Young and Beautiful by Barbara Cartland and Elinor Glyn
Etiquette for Love and Romance
Barbara Cartland's Book of Health

## General:

Barbara Cartland's Book of Useless Information with a Foreword
by the Earl Mountbatten of Burma.
   (In aid of the United World Colleges)
Love and Lovers (Picture Book)
The Light of Love (Prayer Book)
Barbara Cartland's Scrapbook
(In aid of the Royal Photographic Museum)
Romantic Royal Marriages
Barbara Cartland's Book of Celebrities
Getting Older, Growing Younger

## Verse:

Lines on Life and Love

## Music:

An Album of Love Songs sung with the Royal Philharmonic
Orchestra

## Films:

A Hazard of Hearts
The Lady and the Highwayman
A Ghost in Monte Carlo
A Duel of Hearts

## Cartoons:

Barbara Cartland Romances (Book of Cartoons)
has recently been published in the U.S.A., Great Britain,
and other parts of the world.

### Children:

A Children's Pop-Up Book: "Princess to the Rescue"

### Videos:

A Hazard of Hearts
The Lady and the Highwayman
A Ghost in Monte Carlo
A Duel of Hearts

### Cookery:

Barbara Cartland's Health Food Cookery Book
Food for Love
Magic of Honey Cookbook
Recipes for Lovers
The Romance of Food

### Editor of:

"The Common Problem" by Ronald Cartland (with a preface by
the Rt. Hon. the Earl of Selborne, P.C.)
Barbara Cartland's Library of Love
Library of Ancient Wisdom
"Written with Love" Passionate love letters selected by Barbara
Cartland

### Drama:

Blood Money
French Dressing

### Philosophy:

Touch the Stars

### Radio Operetta:

The Rose and the Violet
(Music by Mark Lubbock) Performed in 1942.

### Radio Plays:

The Caged Bird: An episode in the life of Elizabeth Empress of
Austria. Performed in 1957.